DUT

David Sherman

Keith R.A. DeCandido

eSpec Books by David Sherman

18th Race Series
ISSUE IN DOUBT
IN ALL DIRECTIONS
TO HELL AND REGROUP
(with Keith R.A. DeCandido)

DemonTech Series
DEMONTECH: THE LAST CAMPAIGNS

eSpec Books including David Sherman

DOGS OF WAR REISSUED
BEST OF DEFENDING THE FUTURE
THE WEIRD WILD WEST
AFTER PUNK

eSpec Books by Keith R.A. DeCandido

DRAGON PRECINCT
UNICORN PRECINCT
GOBLIN PRECINCT
GRYPHON PRECINCT
MERMAID PRECINCT
TALES FROM DRAGON PRECINCT
WITHOUT A LICENSE
TO HELL AND REGROUP
(with David Sherman)

eSpec Books including Keith R.A. DeCandido

THE BEST OF BAD-ASS FAERIES
THE BEST OF DEFENDING THE FUTURE
THE SIDE OF GOOD/THE SIDE OF EVIL
FOOTPRINTS IN THE STARS

THE 18th RACE
BOOK 3
TO HELL AND REGROUP

DAVID SHERMAN
KEITH R.A. DeCANDIDO

eBooks
Pennsville, NJ

PUBLISHED BY
eSpec Books LLC
Danielle McPhail, Publisher
PO Box 242,
Pennsville, New Jersey 08070
www.especbooks.com

Copyright ©2020 David Sherman

ISBN: 978-1-942990-46-8
ISBN (eBook): 978-1-942990-47-5

All rights reserved. No part of the contents of this book may be reproduced or transmitted in any form or by any means without the written permission of the publisher.

All persons, places, and events in this book are fictitious and any resemblance to actual persons, places, or events is purely coincidental.

Copyediting: Greg Schauer
Design: Mike and Danielle McPhail
Cover Art: Mike McPhail, McP Digital Graphics

This book is dedicated to the memory of:

Sergeant Alvin York

*328th Infantry Regiment
Awarded the Medal of Honor
for action in the Argonne Forest
October 8, 1918*

—David Sherman

To Master Sergeant Charles Keane, U.S. Army Special Forces (ret.), or, as I call him, Senpai Charles. My fellow student of karate, as well as a fellow teacher in our dojo, Senpai Charles and I went for our second-degree and third-degree black-belt promotions together in 2013 and 2017. It's been an honor to train with you, my friend.

—Keith R.A. DeCandido

*Dedicated to the memory of Jeff (Thorir) Scott, super-fan.
Ever patient, ever loyal, and ever missed.
(6/26/56 - 4/29/20)*

—All of us at eSpec Books

ACKNOWLEDGEMENTS

THE AUTHORS WOULD LIKE TO THANK ESPEC BOOKS PUBLISHERS DANIELLE Ackley-McPhail, Mike McPhail, and Greg Schauer for rescuing this trilogy, republishing *Issue in Doubt* and *In All Directions*, and publishing this final book.

Thanks also to Dayton Ward—Marine and author extraordinaire—for casting a watchful eye over the manuscript.

"Marines don't die—they go to hell and regroup."
—old Marine Corps aphorism

The Prairie Palace, Omaha,
Douglas County, Federal Zone,
North American Union

Doctor Julia Gaujot sat, waiting and nervous, outside the office of the North American Union President. While Gaujot had done a significant amount of work for the government, from internships while at graduate school all the way to various government projects on other worlds, she'd never actually been to the Federal Zone before. A New Yorker born and bred, she spent most of her time these days either in the lab at Stony Brook University or on other worlds studying the ruins and fossils of alien civilizations.

"You okay?" the tall, wiry dark-skinned man sitting next to her asked.

Gaujot shook her head. "Not really. I mean, I'm having a meeting with the *president*. It's a very strange ending to a very strange month."

"I getcha." He held out a hand. "Doctor Travis Atkins."

"Doctor Julia Gaujot." She returned the handshake.

Gaujot and Atkins were seated on a bench opposite a large desk occupied by a small woman. That woman touched her ear, then said, "Yes, sir." She looked over at the two doctors. "The president will be ready for you shortly."

"Um, okay," Gaujot said nervously.

Atkins smiled. "Deadly, t'anks."

The double doors to the Round Office opened and an unfamiliar face poked out between the doors. This was probably the Secretary of War, Richmond P. Hobson. Gaujot had been dealing exclusively with Hobson's chief of staff, Joseph Gion, up until today.

"Doctor Gaujot, Doctor Atkins, I'm Secretary Hobson," he said, confirming his identity, "come in please."

They both rose and followed Hobson into a place that was previously seen by Gaujot only on vid screens.

While the president's desk was on the far side of the room, it remained unoccupied at present, with several people seated nearby around a rectangular table.

One of the curved walls of the room had a large screen, which included several images that Gaujot recognized, as she had forwarded them to the Prairie Palace before she left Stony Brook.

At the table itself sat seven people. On one side were four men in uniform. One woman and one man in suits faced them. Hobson moved to sit next to the man. At the foot of the table stood two empty chairs, which were obviously meant for Atkins and Gaujot.

At the head, of course, was President Albert Leopold Mills, who stood up as they entered.

Everyone around the table did likewise.

"Mr. President," Hobson said, "this is Doctor Julie Gaujot of Stony Brook University in New York and Doctor Travis Atkins of Memorial University in St. John's."

Gaujot cast her gaze downward, frightened to look the president in the eye, equally frightened to correct Hobson's mispronunciation of her family name. He'd been saying "GAW-jot" when it was actually pronounced "GOW-joh." But she'd already heard every conceivable pronunciation of her family name over the course of her life and had grown weary of correcting it in any event. And she certainly wasn't going to correct one of the most powerful people on the planet.

"Welcome to the Prairie Palace, Doctors," Mills said with the congenial smile that Gaujot knew full well from the man's presidential addresses.

"Thank you, sir," Gaujot muttered.

"T'anks," Atkins said more loudly, with a broad smile. "It's an honor to be here."

Hobson then performed the introductions, starting with the three military men. "This is Admiral Ira Clinton Welborn, Chairman of the Joint Chiefs of Staff, General John C. Robinson, the Army Chief of Staff, General Ralph Talbot, Commandant of the Marine Corps."

All three nodded to the two doctors. Gaujot gave a quick nod back, while Atkins's smile grew even broader.

To the civilian side of the table, Hobson said, "Jose Nisperos, the President's Chief of Staff, and Secretary of State Mary Walker. I, of course, am Secretary of War Richmond Hobson."

Unlike the others, Hobson put out a hand, and first Gaujot, then Atkins shook it.

Mills took his seat, and then everyone else did likewise. Hobson took the seat next to Walker. Gaujot hesitated before taking the seat next to Atkins at the foot of the table.

"You haven't met Secretary Hobson before?" Mills asked Gaujot. There was an undertone of menace to the president's voice, as though he'd been under the impression that Hobson had been the one to bring these two in on the Duster problem.

"No, sir," Gaujot said, "I've only spoken to the secretary's chief of staff, Mr. Gion?"

Seemingly satisfied, Mills nodded. "Of course. Now I know that Mr. Hobson's office has told you all of this already, and I know that you signed non-disclosure agreements, but I'm going to repeat what you probably know from both of those—the work you have done on our behalf is classified at the highest level. You are to speak to no one of any of this outside this room, and all reports that you have made and will make will remain encrypted and eyes-only. Is that understood?"

"Yes, sir," Atkins said quickly, his smile having modulated into a more serious expression.

Gaujot simply nodded.

"Good. Now, I understand, Doctor Gaujot, that you are a xenobiologist and that you have been studying the alien bodies that were sent back from Troy?"

"Yes, sir," Gaujot said.

"These lovely pictures on my wall are from your analyses, yes?"

Again, Gaujot said, "Yes, sir."

The screen on the wall showed one of the aliens who had invaded Troy. The so-called "Dusters" had heads that were angled down and forward, with long jaws filled with sharp teeth, sitting atop long, sinuous necks. At a resting position, the aliens' torsos tended to run parallel to the ground, bent at the neck above and the hips below, a crest of feathers running from the top of the head down to the hips. Their legs were thick and ended in taloned feet, knees bending backward.

"What is it you have to tell us about our enemy, Doctor?"

"It's about how they reproduce, sir." Gaujot blew out a breath and started the speech she'd been mentally rehearsing since she got on the plane that took her from Long Island to Omaha this morning. "Based on the tests we've run and the autopsies we've performed on the alien bodies, we have come to the preliminary conclusion that they are hermaphrodites and that they reproduce asexually."

Welborn leaned forward. "You're saying they don't mate?"

"Yes, sir, I am saying that. They appear to be fertile instantly and can produce a plenitude of eggs. Each of the bodies had blastocysts developing, and one had an egg nearly complete."

"How many eggs in a plenitude, exactly?" Walker asked.

"It's impossible to know without observing a living specimen in their native habitat. I don't suppose any of the reports from Troy have mentioned eggs?"

Welborn shook his head. "Negative, but the Marines and soldiers on the ground haven't been looking for that in particular—nor, I might add, is there any reason for them to do so now."

"Agreed, Sir, my apologies," Gaujot said quickly, "I was merely asking in the hopes of confirmation."

"So your theory," Hobson said, "is that they reproduce at will?"

"It's more of a hypothesis than a theory, Mr. Secretary, given how little data we have to go on. But I think it's a viable one. It also indicates a massive population, one far greater than humans can create, especially since they're also tool users and creators of technology, which will enable them to enhance that reproductive process. In fact, one of the corpses had a device implanted inside it that seems designed to inject hormones into the body. I saw no such device on any other alien, which leads me to think that this particular being had a need for artificial medical enhancement in order to reproduce."

"I see," Mills said. "Thank you, Doctor. There's an old saying that says you should know your enemy, and you've given us more of that knowledge. The NAU appreciates your efforts."

"Those efforts are still ongoing, sir," Gaujot said.

The President frowned, and Gaujot belatedly realized that his words were a subtle way of saying she was done talking now.

"My apologies, sir," she said quickly, "I merely wished to state that we will know more as time goes on."

"Of course, Doctor." Mills gave those three words a new undercurrent of menace. "Now then, Doctor Atkins, you're one of our foremost experts in xenopsychology, and I'm told you have a report based on Doctor Gaujot's findings."

"Yessir," Atkins said. "Based on both the doctor's findings and on the reports we've gotten back from Troy about the enemy tactics."

Welborn bridled. "Are you an expert on military tactics, Doctor Atkins?"

He grinned again. "Expert? No, but I did serve in the NAU Navy for a six-year bit. Growin' up in Newfoundland, bein' on the water was always a part'a my life." Atkins cleared his throat, as his Newfie accent had gotten thicker with that last sentence.

Welborn was placated by knowing that Atkins had served. "Carry on."

"One common theme in the reports we've gotten so far is that the Dusters have been attacking without any regard to their personal safety. They've sacrificed hundreds in order to achieve their goals in combat. And I think that Doctor Gaujot's hypothesis indicates a cultural bias. See, us humans, we try to live. Even sailors, soldiers, airmen, and Marines do their best to stay alive. We're willin' to sacrifice ourselves if we have to, but it's a last resort for us, even people who're servin'.

"I don't think that's the case for the Dusters. They don't have the same self-preservation instinct that we got. An' I think that the fact that they breed like bunnies is part of it. They're not the type to care much about individual lives, long as the greater good's achieved."

Nisperos folded his hands on the table. "So what you're saying is that the Dusters have a much different notion of acceptable losses in terms of casualties than we do?"

"Pretty much, b'y. Uhm, sir," he added quickly. "The Dusters'll die in the hundreds, even thousands, just to achieve an objective. Their attitude is prob'ly that they can just make a whole lot more."

"Obviously," Nisperos said slowly, "this is not a tactic that we can adapt. And it does go some way toward explaining how the other seventeen races we've found got wiped out by these guys."

"Perhaps, Jose," Welborn said, "but they also never had to face the NAU Navy, Army, and Marines before. We've held our own against them, and even they can't reproduce forever."

"For all we know," Gaujot said, "they have people selected specifically for breeding back on their homeworld to birth more soldiers. Without any idea of their population—"

Hobson held up a hand. "It doesn't matter. This is useful information, but I don't see how it changes anything. Hell, it's information that the people on site already have. We know how they fight—we just have to fight back."

"They'll know they were in a fight, that's for damn sure," Welborn said.

Mills stood up, and so did everyone else a second later. "Doctor Atkins, Doctor Gaujot, thank you both."

"It's our honor, Mr. President," Gaujot said quietly, while Atkins just smiled.

✪

Hobson led the two of them to the door and then left them in the care of the president's secretary.

Mills sat back down, and everyone else took their seats. Hobson did so once he was sure that the two scientists were taken care of.

"Is there any other business?" Mills asked the question in a manner that indicated that he didn't want there to be any other business.

Which explained why Admiral Welborn sounded pained when he replied with: "I'm sorry to say there is, Mr. President. I've got a reporter from the Omaha World-Herald cooling her heels in my office."

The president sighed. "Which one?"

"Florence Groberg."

Another sigh, but it was less resigned. "That's something. She generally knows her ass from her elbow. Didn't she serve?"

Welborn nodded. "Yes, Mr. President, she captained a SEAL boat for two tours before she took her honorable discharge and became a reporter. She's always been savvy to the military POV, which puts her one up on most *World-Herald* word jockeys."

That impressed Mills. She may not have been a SEAL, but she still would have had to go through the training to qualify to run a boat for the SEALs.

Which was good, because the *World-Herald* was mostly a pain in his ass. He had always respected the paper—which had become the premier source for political reporting ever since the NAU formed and established its capital in Omaha—right up until he was elected.

Welborn said, "Unfortunately, she knows everything."

"We have a leak?" Nisperos asked. The chief of staff sounded more than a little concerned.

Sounding much less concerned, Welborn replied, "I'd say we've got several. Groberg's got a *lot* of good sources."

"Honestly," Walker said, "I'm stunned we've kept a lid on for this long. An operation the size of this is incredibly difficult to keep secret, especially out in space. I figured if it did get out, it would be from some kid with a telescope."

Mills gave the secretary of state a derisive look, but then General Talbot said, "She's right. There's no cover out in space—it's why we call it 'space.' And we had to take the most direct route to the wormhole terminus, and you *know* there are civilians out there who look at that route regularly from their back yards. Even a cheap store-bought telescope might see something, and most of these hobbyists have the fancy ones. We could hardly stop them. We were very lucky that it didn't leak that way."

"Is she running the story?" Hobson asked.

"She's playing her cards pretty close to the vest," Welborn said. "I got called into this meeting before we could really get into it. She's a smart cookie. I'm willing to bet dollars to donuts that she's gonna make a very compelling constitutional argument as to why she should run the story."

With another sigh, Mills asked, "I don't suppose we can muzzle her?"

Nisperos shook his head. "Not legally. And truly, not sensibly, either. All we'll do is make an enemy of one of the best and friendliest reporters who cover the Prairie Palace beat. There's no upside, and if Groberg has the story now, the lesser reporters will have it in three or four days, and they *won't* be considerate enough to check in with Admiral Welborn first."

Walker nodded in agreement. "We should get out in front of this. Do a press conference, tell the public everything we can."

Talbot said, "We knew this day was going to come eventually, and Secretary Walker is right, it'll be disastrous if the press tells the public before we do."

"Agreed." Mills turned to Welborn. "Admiral, give her whatever she needs to hold off on the story until after that press conference."

"Yes, Mr. President."

"I assume our esteemed communications director and press secretary have a strategy?" he asked, referring to, respectively, David Bellavia and Clinton Romesha.

"David's had a speech ready for a month now," Nisperos said. "He's been updating it, but it's ready to go, just needs your okay to lock it. And Clint can have the press room ready to go in a matter of minutes."

"Good. Have David send me the speech, and we'll do the press conference first thing tomorrow."

"Mr. President," Walker said hesitantly.

"Yes, Mary?"

"We should inform the families of the citizens of Troy tonight. They shouldn't find out their loved ones are dead from a press conference."

Mills nodded. "Agreed. Let's get it done."

✪

Admiral Welborn entered his office to see the tall, athletic form of Florence Groberg. She may not have been with the SEALs any longer, but she still looked like she kept herself in shape. Welborn respected that—most journalists lived sedentary lives and were significantly rounder around the middle by the time they reached Groberg's age.

She was staring at the east wall of Welborn's office, covered with images of warships from the eighteenth century forward. The wall included drawings, photographs, lithographs, paintings, and holograms from colonial frigates to the latest spaceships and everything in between.

At present, Groberg was studying a black-and-white photograph of two submarine chasers from the early twentieth century.

"SC-43 and SC-44," she said. "Commissioned during the war to end all wars, and then used extensively in the war after that one."

Welborn snorted. He also was not that impressed. The boats were clearly labeled with their designations in large white characters, and the quality of the photograph indicated that it was the early twentieth century.

Groberg went on. "Submarine chasers, designed to go after German U-boats in both wars, and Japanese ones, too, in the latter war. Based on British designs, but significantly improved on them." She finally turned to face Welborn. "They didn't look like much, certainly not something that could take on a behemoth like a German sub, but they were fast, and they were efficient, and they got the job done."

Now Welborn was impressed—both with her knowledge of military history and her not-so-subtle metaphor. "Sorry to keep you waiting, Ms. Groberg. Have a seat."

Even as Groberg sat back down in the guest chair, Welborn sat in the plush leather chair behind his large desk.

"So, before you were called away, you were about to give me the national security speech, right?" Groberg said with a grin.

"You do understand that this mission is classified, yes?"

"The Semi-Autonomous World of Troy has been wiped out by an alien invasion force, and the NAU has responded with a massive tactical response the likes of which has not been seen since SC-43 and SC-44 up there were decommissioned." Groberg waved a hand at the photograph she'd been admiring. "Do the families of the people killed even know what has happened?"

"It's being dealt with," Welborn said neutrally.

Groberg's face hardened. "That would be no, then."

"I can't divulge—"

"Admiral, before you dig yourself deeper, I've spoken to several relatives of people who live on Troy—don't worry, I didn't give anything away. I spoke to them on the pretense of a story about having family living on other worlds. Every single one of them thinks their family member is alive and well and living on Troy. Now I understand why you kept a lid on this to start—you didn't know what was going on, and you didn't want to tell people that a colony world was wiped out without knowing who or what did it.

"But we're past the point where that even makes sense anymore. I know we've engaged an alien species on Troy and that the fighting has been brutal. And I know how easy it is to fall into the cycle of secrecy."

"Excuse me?" Welborn said angrily, not liking the way the conversation was going.

"It starts with keeping it a secret because we don't know anything and don't want people to speculate. But that feeds on itself, and you keep it a secret because you've already kept mum about it so long and people will ask why you've kept it quiet, and on and on and on. It has to stop sometime."

"Can the palaver, Ms. Groberg, and kindly tell me what you want in exchange for sitting on this story until the president's press conference tomorrow morning."

Groberg grinned. "Oh, so there will be a press conference?"

"Yes. And the families will be notified before that, rest assured. So—what do you want?"

"Ten minutes with the president."

Welborn snorted. "No chance. I can give you the first question tomorrow morning, and I'll even talk on the record about the operation after the conference, but—"

"I'll take both those things, but I still want ten minutes with the president. I'll send my questions ahead of time, and you'll have full veto power over them, but this is not negotiable. If my editor knows I sat on this for a week—"

"You've had it for a *week*?" Welborn sputtered.

"Bits of it—it didn't come completely together until yesterday, and I spent last night drinking a significant amount of bourbon while trying to figure out whether or not to run it or come to you first."

For the first time since he came into the office, Welborn smiled. "Always admired the magical properties of a good glass of bourbon."

Groberg snorted. "Five good glasses, but yes. In either case, the only way I keep my job after not telling my boss about this is if I get an exclusive with President Mills. So that's my price, and it's *not* negotiable."

Welborn sighed. The president *did* say to give her whatever she needed.

He stood up and held out a hand. "Done."

Groberg also rose and returned the handshake. "Excellent." Her face softened. "I understand that you lost Task Force 7. I'm sorry."

"Thank you, but you can rest assured that all our losses will be avenged. Troy will be ours again, you can count on that."

Admiral's Bridge, Battleship NAUS Durango,
in geosync orbit around Semi-Autonomous World Troy

Rear Admiral James Avery, commander of the North American Union Navy's Task Force 8, studied the big board, which covered most of the bridge's forward bulkhead and displayed all the elements on both sides. He watched the tiny flecks that indicated the SF 6 Meteor space-fighters as they launched from the carrier *Rear Admiral Norman Scott*, formed up, then headed for their targets: the leading ships of the approaching alien fleet, forty enemy vessels to TF 8's eight warships.

When the Meteors were a third of the way to the enemy, Avery said, "Laser batteries, fire on my mark."

Avery didn't see Captain Harry M.P. Huse standing behind him as he replied, "Laser batteries, stand by." The admiral was completely focused on the tactical display on the big board.

Lieutenant Commander George F. Davis spoke *sotto voce* into his headset, transmitting Avery's orders to the three destroyers in TF 8.

"Laser batteries standing by," said the voice of Chief Petty Officer Henry Finkenbiner.

When the Meteors were halfway to their destination, Avery said, simply, "Fire."

"Laser batteries, fire," Huse said much louder, enough to echo off the bulkheads.

Finkenbiner said, "Laser batteries firing."

Beams of coherent light burst forth from the *Durango*. A moment later, TF 8's three destroyers fired their lasers as well, carrying out the same fire order, relayed by Davis.

Lasers lanced out from the second rank of the enemy fleet, the alien equivalent of battleships and cruisers.

Avery ordered his three frigates, stationed above and to the left of the enemy, to attack the second rank.

TF 8 achieved several hits on the bogeys, which appeared on the board as glowing red splotches.

Avery looked on stoically as enemy lasers converged on the destroyer *First Lieutenant George H. Cannon*, and she erupted, her spine split through and her missile magazine exploded. Debris scattered everywhere.

Multiple laser hits struck the Durango's hull. Horns sounded, signaling damage control teams into action.

The *Scott's* four Meteor squadrons closed to range and opened fire on the leading rank of alien warships, their version of frigates and destroyers.

The enemy fleet opened fire on the fighters, killing many of them. The only evident damage the Meteors had done was one warship in the leading rank lost weight.

Another of TF 8's destroyers was killed, as was one of the frigates.

"Sir," Davis said, "the bogey fleet seems to be accelerating."

The fast attack carrier Rear Admiral Isaac C. Kidd, approaching the flank of the alien fleet

"This shouldn't be any more difficult than when we acted as a screen for ARG 17," Captain John P. Cromwell, the *Kidd's* Commander Air Group, said at the end of his mission briefing. "Now get out there and kick some alien ass. Catfish first, followed by Lionfish."

He strode from the briefing room, trying very hard not to think about how few of his pilots remained after the fight to save Amphibious Ready Group 17. They had what they had, and they would fight to the end, regardless.

"Catfish, let's go!" Lieutenant Adolphus Staton, the commander of VSF 114 Catfish squadron snapped. He led his pilots to the launch bay. Only twelve of the squadron's original sixteen pilots remained, and only ten of them had usable fighter craft.

In the launch bay, the pilots, heading out on what they feared might be a suicide mission, quickly ran pre-flight checks on their SF 6 Meteors and mounted up. By the time the Meteors of VSF 114 began trundling to the launch tube, the remaining pilots of VSF 218 Lionfish were engaged in their pre-flights.

In minutes the two truncated squadrons were linked together in echelon left formation, with Catfish in the lead. They blasted toward the flank of the rear rank of alien warcraft.

"They're dropping back," Lieutenant Abraham DeSomer, Lionfish's commander, said into the joint squadron freq.

"Stand by for new vector," Staton replied, his fingers dancing over his tac-comp's controls. In seconds, he transmitted a course adjustment to the two dozen Meteors, putting them on a firing line for the closest ships in the enemy's rear rank. He watched his tactical display as the two squadrons closed on their targets.

"On my mark," he said when the comp showed the space closing to effective range, "Lionfish, lead the nearer ship with Beanbags. Catfish, fire Zappers at the second."

He began a countdown.

"Ten."

Staton found his mind going back to when he first signed up.

"Nine."

In particular, he remembered something Sergeant Frank Fratanellico told him during training.

"Eight."

"You're not you anymore," Sergeant Fratanellico had said back then.

"Seven."

"Once you climb into the cockpit, you're not Adolphus Staton, you're the fighter."

"Six."

"You're the brain, and the fighter's the body that does what you tell it to do."

"Five."

Fratanellico had pointed a thick finger right at Staton's face at the next part.

"Four."

"You'll know you're a *real* pilot the moment you and the fighter react as fast as your body does to your brain's commands."

"Three."

Staton had found that Fratanellico was right—by the time he had become CAG, the Meteor and he were in perfect sync.

"Two."

He hoped that was enough today against the Dusters.

"One. *Mark!*"

Staton's Meteor lurched when a missile shot out from its bay on its underside. He effortlessly keyed in commands for his tac-comp to calculate a vector to a different target, and the Meteor responded instantly, just like Sergeant Fratanellico said it would.

A moment later, glittering puffs appeared in front of the nearest alien ship. The vessel staggered and began tumbling when it slammed into the sand and gravel the Beanbags scattered in its path. The particulates blocked visual and also got into the machinery, causing the Dusters' craft to seize up and crash. Seconds later, another ship shuddered and spun out of formation when the Zappers from Lionfish squadron blasted out powerful bursts of electromagnetic energy, frying its electronics.

"Two down," Staton murmured to himself. "Twenty to go?" He thought the starships next in line, which appeared to be dropping into planetfall trajectories, must be transports.

He also knew the math was never going to work here. The air group could take down some of the Duster ships, but a mess of them were going to get through to land on Troy.

But they kept fighting. Something else Fratanellico had said back then: "You don't stop fighting until ten minutes after you're dead. And maybe not even then."

Admiral's Bridge, NAUS Durango

Rear Admiral Avery, watching his big board, saw the trailing ranks of alien ships falling back and heading planetward, and came to the same conclusion as Staton about the math not working.

"Comm," he said to Lieutenant Commander Davis, "notify Commander, NAU Forces, Troy that twenty or more enemy transports are preparing to make planetfall."

"Notify Commander, NAU Forces, Troy that twenty or more enemy transports are preparing to make planetfall, aye," Davis said, and made the call.

Headquarters, North American Union Forces,
near Millerton, Shapland
Semi-Autonomous World Troy

"Sir."

Lieutenant General Harold Bauer, commander of the 1st Marine Combat Force and acting commander of NAU Forces, Troy, looked away from the display he was studying of the battle going on in orbit.

"Yes, Bill?" he asked, seeing his aide, Captain William Upshur, standing in the doorway of his office.

"A message from orbit, Sir." When Bauer nodded, Upshur continued. "The rear echelons of the Duster fleet have dropped into planetfall orbits. It appears that half of them are headed for Shapland, and the rest to Eastern Shapland."

"Get my major element commanders on conference."

"Aye aye, Sir." Upshur about-faced and went to do his commander's bidding.

In moments, images of the commanding generals of the 1st Marine Division, the 2nd Marine Air Wing, the Army's 9th Infantry Division, and the independent commands under NAUF-T came up on Bauer's display.

"Gentlemen," Bauer said brusquely, "the moment is upon us. Twenty-odd Duster ships are dropping into planetfall orbit. We should expect them to begin launching landing craft at any time. Make sure you are linked into the Navy's tracking feed so you can follow the shuttles' movements once they launch, and when they make planetfall.

"One-oh-fourth Arty, as soon as the ships come into your laser batteries' range, start taking them out. Marine artillery, kill the landing craft with your lasers.

"Force Recon, I want eyeballs on the lead Duster elements.

"Second Marine Air Wing, get Kestrels aloft, ready to strike targets of opportunity as identified by NavInt and FR eyes.

"Everybody, stand by to kick some Duster ass. Bauer out."

Headquarters, 1st Marine Division,
near Jordan, Eastern Shapland

Major General Hugh Purvis turned from the blanked display of the just-ended conference call to look at his staff and major subordinate commanders. Before the call with Bauer, they had either been watching the tactical display from space coming in or just looking up into the sky. There had been flashes and blossoms of actinic light speckling and freckling the night sky over the past few hours as TF 8 and the alien warships went at it. It might have made an impressive display under better circumstances.

"Gentlemen," Purvis said, "if any of you had any residual uncertainty, now you know what the light show we've been admiring was all about. The fight is about to pass to us."

His gaze fixed on First Lieutenant John A. Hughes, commander of the first section of the Force Recon platoon.

"Go find 'em, Lieutenant."

"Aye aye, *Sir*," Hughes said, and turned to gather his Marines.

Nobody asked why Force Recon had to go find the Dusters when Navy intelligence was watching them from orbit. They all understood that a Marine with his boots on the ground might see and understand details that the Navy eye-in-the-sky might miss. Besides, the Navy had its own fight above, and comm with planetside could be broken.

Firebase Westermark, Eastern Shapland

Corporal Denise Conlan sat tensely at the controls for the long-range laser batteries that had been emplaced in Eastern Shapland.

Next to her, Corporal Horace Carswell regarded the scanners, waiting for the Dusters to come into range.

The pair of them had trained together and worked together for several months now, and they had achieved an impressive reputation for accuracy and speed. The rest of the unit called them "C&C," though the brass objected to the nickname's similarity to the abbreviation for Command and Control.

The brass, typically, missed the point. The nickname stuck *because* of the homonym, not despite it.

"Think the Marines'll be able to take them out?" Carswell asked Conlan.

"They can try," Conlan said. "But those wussy-ass guns they're firing couldn't light a firecracker, much less dust a Duster. Don't worry, though, when those jarheads screw the pooch, we'll be there to show 'em how it's done."

Carswell smiled. "Damn right."

Then the smile fell as his scanners started to beep several alarms. "Bogeys coming in!"

The voice of Marine Sergeant William Doolen sounded over both of C&C's comms. "Preparing to fire batteries. We got these—"

Doolen cut himself off, and Carswell saw why immediately: the Dusters' course was taking them a hundred klicks from Eastern Shapland, completely out of the batteries' range.

"No firing solution," Doolen said quickly, "I say again, Marines have no firing solution."

Carswell grinned. "Wussy-ass is right. Their lasers'll be flashlights by the time they reach the bad guys."

"Line 'em up," Conlan said. "Let's show them how we do things in the Army."

"Acquiring target now," Carswell said with a grin.

Then, for the second time in five minutes, he lost his grin. "Enemy changing course! Dammit! Out of range!"

"Sonofabitch!"

Doolen's voice came over the comms. "Looks like the Dusters made monkeys out of all of us."

Conlan and Carswell watched as the Dusters landed well out of everyone's range.

"What the hell're they planning?" Carswell asked.

"Staying out of range of our batteries, forcing us to engage them on the ground. I guess they figure they have a better shot at hand-to-hand, even after moving on dirt for an hour to get to where the fight is instead of just landing right here."

"Well, we would've taken them out if they landed closer."

"Exactly. Probably cost 'em some casualties, and then there's the effort of hauling ass all the way here from where they're landing."

Carswell frowned. "You think it's a smart strategy, Corporal?"

Shrugging, Conlan said, "The only smart strategy is the one that works. And we ain't gonna find that out until it's all over."

Firebase Gasson,
near Millerton, Shapland,
Semi-Autonomous World Troy

SECOND LIEUTENANT THEODORE W. GREIG AND SERGEANT FIRST CLASS Alexander M. Quinn, commander and platoon sergeant of second platoon, Alpha Company, First of the Seventh Mounted Infantry, left the command bunker and headed for an open area in the firebase. First Lieutenant Archie Miller of the Ninth Mobile Intel Company trailed them.

"Second platoon, gather around," Quinn shouted.

In moments, the forty men of the second were grouped in front of their commander and sergeant.

"Troops," Greig began, "we're about to begin earning our pay—again. It looks like Duster troop ships are shortly going to drop landing craft near the Marines on Eastern Shapland. It also appears that another flotilla of troop ships will head toward us. Very shortly," he waved a hand toward the laser in the center of the firebase, "the arty will be getting ready. Maybe they can kill some of the ships before they drop their landing craft on us. Certainly, they can kill some of the landing craft before they land their troops. We need to be ready to fight them and defeat them once they land and we are in the thick of things. We fought them before, and we beat their asses when we did. We'll do it again."

"But!" He paused and gave his men a hard look. "That doesn't mean it's going to be easy. Don't think that these Dusters don't know what's already happened here. Don't think that, because they're new, they're dumb. There's a damn good chance they learned from the mistakes made by the ones we already beat. We have to be ready in case this new alien army uses different, less suicidal tactics." He took a deep breath. "We know they can kill us. That's how our firebases got their names."

Several of the troops lowered their heads. Gasson, Cart, and Garrett were all soldiers from Alpha Troop who had been killed by the Dusters.

Greig continued: "Once the Dusters make planetfall, I'm sure our friends in Mobile Intel will let us know where they're coming from, and what their strength is." That last was said with a glance at Miller.

In response, Miller gave the platoon a confident thumb's up.

"In the meanwhile, squad leaders see the platoon sergeant. He'll make sure your squads have enough ammunition to defeat a Duster battalion."

Someone in the platoon muttered loudly enough for everyone to hear, "One platoon against a battalion? Mamas, don't let your sons grow up to be soldiers." At least a few soldiers developed quick coughing fits to cover their laughter.

Greig studiously ignored it, which stopped even the coughing. He turned to Quinn. "Sergeant, the platoon is yours."

"Yes, Sir." Quinn faced him and saluted. Greig returned the salute and headed back to the command bunker.

"All right," Quinn said as soon as the officer was far enough away, "squad leaders, check your men's ammo and report back to me how much they have so I can get you up to snuff. Dismissed."

Even as he said the words, he thought, *Enough ammo to defeat a battalion? If we have to fight that many, we won't live long enough to use it all.*

The squad leaders took their soldiers to their bunkers to inspect their ammunition supplies, and returned with their reports in just a few minutes.

"First squad has fifteen thousand rounds," Staff Sergeant Albert O'Connor said.

Quinn grimaced. If everybody had a similar amount of ammunition, they didn't have nearly enough to beat off a battalion—even if the new Dusters used the same suicidal tactics as the ones already on Troy used.

Staff Sergeant Alphonso Lunt reported, "Two has fourteen-five." He didn't look any happier than O'Connor did.

"Third's got a bit more than fifteen," Staff Sergeant Charles Breyer said. He looked and sounded more stoic than the other two, but Quinn figured he was just as displeased.

Staff Sergeant Sydney Gumpertz, the machine gun squad leader, muttered, "Guns never have enough."

Quinn looked at the three rifle squad leaders. "Sounds like some of your boys have been hoarding. I'll try to get you up to twenty each. Twenty-five if I can. As for you," he looked at Gumpertz, "that tells me squat about how much you *do* have. Try again."

Gumpertz shrugged. "At rapid-fire, we can keep going for not much more than twenty minutes. A couple of hours at slow-fire. But the way those bastards jink and jive, we need rapid-fire most of the time. Oh, and extra barrels, 'cause we'll be melting them like butter if we have to shoot that much that fast."

"You're right, you don't have enough. If we go up against a battalion, we'll be fighting all day, all night, and maybe into the next day." *If we live that long.* He repressed a shiver. "What about grenades?"

Each staff sergeant reported their supply, which wound up to an average of six per soldier.

Quinn nodded. "I'll double that. Now, I need a work detail to go with me to pick up the ammo. Squad leaders, assign one man each. I'll tell the LT what we need, and see about getting a truck. Anything else?"

Gumpertz raised a hand. "Yeah, how do we get outta this chicken outfit?"

Several soldiers chuckled, but Quinn's face hardened. "Feet first. Anything else that isn't nonsense?"

The chucklers clammed up, and everyone else remained quiet. "Good. Dismissed."

Inside the Command Bunker;
Firebase Gasson

Captain Patricia H. Pentzer, commander of fourth platoon, H Company, 1045 Artillery Battalion (Laser), watched the reports coming in from her battalion headquarters and the HQ of First of the Seventh with keen attention. She wanted to know the moment the alien fleet started dropping landing shuttles.

Across the way, Quinn was telling Grieg what he needed.

"How much do we have in the platoon's ammo bunker?" Greig asked. "Just in case they won't give us as much as we ask for."

"We're down to seventy-five thousand rifle rounds and the same number for the guns, along with a couple hundred grenades."

"'Down'?" Greig frowned.

Quinn nodded. "I was concerned that some of the troops were hoarding. Some of them probably raided the ammo bunker to beef up what they had. That seventy-five is about twenty-five percent less than what we had on my last inspection."

Pentzer snorted. Soldiers were *always* sneaking off with extra ammo, like a junkie going for a fix. She knew because she'd done it plenty in her time in service.

"All right, Sergeant," Greig said. "I'll also get you that truck."

"Thank you, Sir."

"Dismissed."

Quinn retreated from the command bunker to summon the M117 Growler armored personnel carriers.

Greig walked over to where Pentzer was watching the display.

"They're coming," she said.

One hour later

The first shuttle craft started dropping in the area of the Marines on Eastern Shapland. In another moment, it became evident that the Dusters were dropping half of their forces there, and sending the rest to Shapland—and Pentzer's platoon.

"Fourth platoon, man guns!" Pentzer cried as she raced out of the bunker. Greig and Quinn were right behind her, calling for second platoon.

First Sergeant James Llewellyn P. Norton, the H Battery platoon's top dog, stepped outside the bunker and bellowed the same command as he dashed to a nearby Major Mite quarter-ton truck.

Throughout the firebase, artillerymen stopped whatever they were doing and scrambled to their guns.

"Man guns, man guns, man guns!" Pentzer snapped into her comm on the platoon freq.

"Where to, Top?" Corporal Joseph Fisher asked as he hopped into the Major Mite.

"Cart first, then Garrett," Norton answered as he climbed in and grabbed the dash-bar—he knew how manically Fisher drove when he was in a hurry. The way the platoon commander and top sergeant had shouted their orders, the driver knew he had to go fast.

"Cart, then Garrett," Fisher repeated. "On the way!"

The small truck lurched as he slammed the accelerator, the vehicle raised a rooster tail of dust and debris as it headed out the gate and turned right to Firebase Cart, a kilometer distant.

When they arrived, they found the ten-strong laser crew already in place, and the gun captain, First Lieutenant William H. Newman, on his comm being briefed by Pentzer. Norton gave the laser and its crew a quick inspection with Master Sergeant David Ayers, the assistant gun captain. Satisfied that all was in readiness, he gave Newman a quick glance to determine that the gun captain was still being briefed, then climbed back into the Major Mite and grabbed hold.

Fisher spun out, heading for Garrett.

There, they found First Lieutenant Abram P. Haring just finished with Pentzer's briefing.

Norton snapped a quick salute. "Everything ready, Mr. Haring?"

"As ready as we can be, Top," Haring said. He turned to his assistant, Master Sergeant Henry Fox. "Right, Sergeant?"

"You got it," Fox replied. "All we need is targets."

"You'll have targets soon enough," Norton said. He looked toward the eastern horizon, half expecting to see Duster troop ships appearing. He accompanied Haring and Fox in an inspection of the laser and its crew. All was ready.

"Home, James," Norton said when he was again seated in the small truck.

"Sure thing, Boss," Fisher replied with a wide grin. He drove slightly more sedately this time.

Captain Pentzer was back in the bunker, giving fire directions to her guns when they returned. Before ducking in, Norton looked toward the eastern horizon, where he could see the glints of reflected sunlight off enemy spacecraft as they moved into view. The screech of tortured air jabbed at his ears, and he saw a spear of coherent air lance toward the troop ships, joined by spears from the guns at Cart and Garrett. A ragged cheer raised inside Gasson from the soldiers who saw the targeted spacecraft spout atmosphere and begin to lose weight. More cheers rose when small dots of reflected light began dropping off the ship.

Norton didn't cheer; he knew that the smaller dots were probably landing craft being launched from the wounded troop ship. He doubted that they were going to make planetfall at the same place as the rest of the landing force. The soldiers were going to be facing the enemy from two directions.

Camp Jimmie E. Howard,
Home of 1st Section, 1st Force Recon Platoon
Near Jordan, Eastern Shapland

"ALL RIGHT, MARINES," FIRST LIEUTENANT JOHN A. HUGHES SAID AT THE END of his briefing, "you know what to do. Now do it!"

The twenty Marines of the section roared as one: *"Oo-rah, Force Recon!"*

"On me," Gunnery Sergeant Ernest Janson ordered as Hughes marched toward the section's command bunker.

The Force Recon Marines gathered around their top NCO. "You've got your maps, your comms, water and rations, and weapons. Squad leaders, you have your Squad Pod assignments. Now get out there, find 'em and fix 'em so air can fuck 'em before they get here. Anybody got any dumb questions?"

Nobody asked why Gunny Janson said air instead of Navy gunfire—they all knew Marine air would probably have to lay the first fire on the alien enemy because the Navy had its own battle in space and might not be able to launch a planetside bombardment. Nobody asked why Hughes and Janson weren't going, either—they all knew that an officer or senior NCO on patrol with an FR squad would more likely than not be in the way. There weren't any other questions, dumb or otherwise.

"Squad leaders, go to it." Janson came to attention and popped a sharp salute at the men heading into enemy territory.

"First squad, with me!" Staff Sergeant J. Henry Denig shouted, and began moving to the right-most of the four Squad Pods that sat waiting a hundred meters distant. His four men followed briskly.

"Two, let's go!" called Staff Sergeant Andrew Miller, and led his men at a trot to the next Squad Pod in line.

"Third squad, let's beat them!" Staff Sergeant William Bordelon shouted, and began sprinting.

"Ho-ho, Four, go!" Sergeant Joseph Julian roared, and sprinted at the head of his squad, trying to get ahead of the others.

In a minute, the twenty Marines were in their Squad Pods, small anti-grav vehicles capable of flying a Force Recon squad or half an infantry squad in nape-of-the-earth flying, and the vehicles' ramps were closing in preparation for launch.

In Sierra Papa One, Denig pulled out his rolled-up map, snapped it to rigidity, and plugged it into the pod's navigation comp. "Count off," he ordered his men.

Behind him, Sergeant Edward Walker barked, "One, tucked in, J. Henry."

Almost everyone in the section called the staff sergeant "J. Henry." It dated back to Denig's time in Boot Camp when the other Marines kept calling him "Denigrate." Finally, Sergeant Jon Cavaiani, who referred to everyone he trained as "motherfuckers" up until they finished Boot Camp, barked, "You will call him J. Henry, motherfuckers!"

From that moment forward, *everyone* called him "J. Henry."

"Two's beddie-bye," came from Corporal John Rannahan.

Corporal Charles Brown answered, "Three's in, J. Henry."

"Four, bringing up the rear, J. Henry—as usual," Lance Corporal Erwin Boydson said with a trace of ironic sourness.

Walker carried the only rifle in the squad—everyone else had sidearms and knives. He adjusted the rifle's position, only to poke Rannahan in the side with it.

Rannahan yelped. "Watch it, Walker!"

"Sorry 'bout that." Walker didn't sound in the least bit sorry.

Rannahan glared at the sergeant.

Denig glanced at Walker and Rannahan both. "You've got the only offensive weapon in this pod, Sergeant. Use it to poke Dusters, not Marines."

"Sorry, J. Henry." This time, Walker sounded like he meant it.

Satisfied that Walker was sufficiently chastised, the staff sergeant checked the pod's nav display, confirming that the route was programmed in, and switched to his comm's control frequency. "Sierra Papa One, zeroed in and ready to launch."

In another moment, the other three squads reported ready to launch.

Hughes's voice came back, "Foxtrot Romeo One, one through four, launch in sequence."

"Sierra Papa One, launching."

Denig's fingers tapped the launch sequence on the Squad Pod's control panel, and the craft's anti-grav engine came to life, lifting it from the launch pad. At ten meters, high enough to clear the surrounding berm and defensive wire beyond, the transport began moving forward, gaining velocity as it went. A hundred meters farther and it banked shallowly to the right and slowly rose to just above the tops of the tree-like forest growths that began at the edge of the kilometer-wide cleared area that surrounded Howard—the killing zone.

A small screen next to the main control panel showed the other three pods launching in sequence, and turning onto their own courses.

Once over the trees, the Squad Pod began wending its way, keeping as much as possible to the lower areas of the gently undulating landscape. After a flight of little more than half an hour and two hundred kilometers, the pod eased itself into a small clearing created when a bolt of lightning had split a forest giant; the large tree had toppled smaller trees when it fell. The pod's ramp dropped, and the five Marines scrambled off. They dashed in different directions and went to ground facing outward fifty meters from the Squad Pod, each of them making one point of a five-pointed star. They didn't exactly blend into the foliage; their uniforms' camouflage was patterned so as to fool the eye into looking past them, rendering them effectively invisible to any but the most intense gaze. Even the faceplates of their helmets had the eye-tricking pattern on their outer sides, although they allowed unobstructed vision from the inside.

The surrounding forest held of a variety of flora, some spindly, some gnarled and twisty, some bush-like. The foliage wasn't packed as tightly as most that the Marines had seen on other worlds; some of them were basically trees, much taller than the rest, raising more than fifty meters into the air. These had branches that began a couple of meters above the ground, and large leaves that blocked most of the sunlight from reaching the surface. Most of the saplings that managed to sprout between the trees looked weak. There was a light speckling of fern-like fronds amid the fallen leaves and other detritus on the ground.

As soon as he dropped, Denig sent a five-word burst transmission on a tight beam to orbit, where it would be retransmitted to the Force Recon headquarters at Camp Howard, "Foxtrot Romeo One, in place."

"Roger, Foxtrot Romeo One," was the four-word burst reply from Force Recon command.

From that point on, nobody in the squad would say anything else unless the enemy was detected, or until it was time for the squad to move out.

All five of the Marines had motion detectors, set to register anything larger than a mid-sized Earth dog moving within two hundred meters. All five of them also had infrared filters for their helmet plates, allowing them to see heat signatures. Sergeant Walker and Corporal Rannahan also had "sniffers," devices that analyzed organic molecules wafting through the air—in the time the Marines and Army had been on Troy, the Navy science team had isolated the airborne tells that would signal the presence of the Dusters and their smaller companions.

Denig's helmet comm also drew in a feed from orbit, showing the current location of the enemy forces his squad awaited. The feed showed the outliers of the main Duster formation, if the skittery mob advancing toward the Marines could be called a formation.

The forest noises returned to normal after a few minutes. Some daring avians swooped at the Squad Pod, investigating this strange object that had manifested in their territory. More hopped or flitted about, dining on the buzzing and crawling insectoids expressing an interest in colonizing this abruptly new environment.

After twenty minutes, with the nearest Dusters closing to ten kilometers, Denig made his next transmissions. The first was five words to Camp Howard: "Foxtrot One, moving to intercept." The second was one word to his squad: "Online." The message to the squad was over a freq that fizzled to less than a whisper within two hundred and fifty meters. On his command, the five Marines rose from their prone positions and spread out to seventy-five-meter intervals, facing toward where they knew the Dusters were. Denig *beeped* a command to the Squad Pod to close its ramp, which had remained down in case the squad had to leave in a hurry, and launch to a holding position three kilometers above. They moved carefully enough that they didn't disturb the fauna back into silence.

The Marines began advancing until they could hear the approaching Dusters. Then Denig sent another one-word message. "Trees." Each of them went to the nearest forest giant and scrambled up it.

The squad leader scooted halfway up the tree he climbed. The first thing he noticed as he settled onto a branch sturdy enough to support his weight without bending, was the sudden silence from the avians, all of whom seemed to have ceased their flitting and swooping.

Odd, he thought, looking at the feed from orbit. *These Dusters aren't close enough to disturb them.*

A flicker of motion on the ground caught his attention. He peered at it, and saw the form of a Duster, padding softly through the thin undergrowth. Its torso was bent parallel to the ground, the feather-like structures that usually fanned out from its tail were stuck straight behind. In front, its beaked head swung side to side on its long neck. The feathery crest that ran from the aliens' heads to the fan at their tails was invisible, covered by something a low glossy deep brown. *Body armor? That's new.*

Denig thought the thing carried a rifle in its short arms, almost hidden from above by its body. It moved straight ahead at about the speed of a rapidly walking man.

Now Denig checked his motion detector; it showed movement about twenty meters to either side of the alien. A quick visual check confirmed that there were more of the aliens.

Strange, he thought. *They seem to be a skirmish line in advance of their main force. They haven't done that before.* He nodded when he saw that the feed from orbit didn't show the thin line of Dusters passing beneath the trees. *Not enough of a mass for orbit to pick up.*

To make sure, he brought his infra into play and scanned the entire ground area visible from his position. Nothing showed up, other than the Dusters he'd already spotted. These had been quiet, unlike the Dusters he'd heard moments earlier, Dusters that sounded closer now.

He turned all his sensors to the sounds; the muted *caws*, ripping of claws through the detritus on the ground, snapping of treelings, shrill *yelps* and *thuds* from aliens who had tripped and fallen.

And then he saw them.

This was the kind of disorderly mass he'd previously seen. Individual Dusters skittered side to side, dashed ahead, darted backward. Somehow kept moving forward. Their movement too fast for him to aim at, even if he'd been on an interdiction mission rather than reconnaissance. He began seeing small packs of the half-size aliens among the Dusters. These didn't wear the suspected body armor or carry weapons. Their stubby arms stuck out forward and displayed the vicious talons at the ends of their hands.

He hoped the scuttlebutt going around was true—that Lieutenant General Bauer had requested shotguns. Weapons that threw out a spray instead of single bullets would make shooting the manically moving aliens easier for individual riflemen to hit when the shooting began.

Self-propelled carts lumbered among the Dusters, barrels sticking up from them at a forty-five-degree angle. Denig thought they must be the anti-air artillery the aliens had used a few times. He saw nothing that resembled an electronic control unit, which made him suspect the AA was dumb artillery like the guns that had killed an AV 16 (E) aerial reconnaissance plane earlier. The guns looked like their barrels could depress far enough for them to be used as surface-to-surface artillery. Mechanical noises began to clank from behind the mob of Dusters and AA artillery.

Denig gritted his teeth; whatever was coming was too far back for him to make out, even in infrared. He was going to have to wait to see whatever additional new equipment the aliens were bringing to bear on the Marines around Jordan.

He took a deep breath and got his nerves under control. Patience was a virtue that Force Recon Marines had in abundance. It was the first thing that Sergeant Cavaiani had taught them—not how to field-strip a weapon, not how to climb a wall, not the art of hand-to-hand combat. Instead, the first day, Cavaiani had them all stand stock still for an hour in the middle of a field on a hundred-degree day in San Diego. Anyone who moved had to do fifty pushups, and the time it took to do those pushups was added to their time standing still.

"When the bell rings, motherfuckers," Cavaiani had said afterward, "you need to be the best fighters in the damn galaxy. But most of the time you're going to be not moving, not fighting, not doing a goddamn thing. A Marine's life is one part fighting, and ninety-nine parts sitting on your ass waiting to fight. Which means you motherfuckers need to be patient about not doing jackshit."

You'd be proud of us today, Sergeant, Denig thought as he watched the mass of Dusters and trundling carts pass below without noticing the five Marines watching them overhead. Denig recorded them and mentally estimated their numbers.

Hundreds.

Thousands.

Yeah, Lieutenant Hughes's briefing had said that Navy intel estimated the Dusters landed at least a corps-size number of soldiers. The intel didn't say what size corps, but that meant the 1st Marine Regiment was outnumbered at least two to one, probably by more than that. And the Navy hadn't said anything about the AA or whatever it was that clanked ever closer. He didn't dare send a burst of data to orbit; nobody knew what kind of electronic capabilities the Dusters had, or whether they could detect transmissions from nearby, even transmissions directed away from them. If they had that capability and he sent a burst to orbit, Denig and his squad were dead.

He estimated that, if they were more or less uniformly spread or bunched in his squad's area, five thousand Dusters passed below them, along with at least four hundred AA carts and a thousand or more of the dog-sized raveners, before the clanking machines got close enough to appear in infrared. What showed made him blink in surprise.

Tanks?

The Dusters hadn't had armored vehicles of any sort before—certainly not that he'd heard of.

It wasn't long before they were close enough for Denig to see them with his unaided eyes. If the tubes protruding from their fronts were the guns they resembled, the vehicles were tanks, but of a strange design. They didn't appear to have turrets, so the entire vehicle would have to point at its target rather than swivel from side to side as human armor did.

They didn't stay in a disciplined formation, but rather went forward in spurts and jinked side to side, mimicking the movement of the foot soldiers. Some of the soldiers lagged behind the mass of Dusters and Denig thought they were in danger of being run over by their own tanks.

The Marine gave an internal headshake. Artillery mixed in with infantry, followed by armor. That was so counter to how humans would move: put the armor up front supported by infantry, with the artillery bringing up the rear where it could fire over the heads of the infantry and armor.

I guess we call them alien for a reason, he thought.

When the last of the armored vehicles finally clanked past, Denig allowed another ten minutes for any stragglers to come along before he was satisfied they were all gone. Then he sent burst messages to his men, asking what they'd seen. Their reports confirmed the numbers he'd already estimated. It was only the work of another minute to prepare a transmission to orbit, to be forwarded to the Force Recon command group at Camp Howard. He included the vids from all of his men. Then one more message to his men:

"Dismount." As he began climbing down the tree, he beeped another message to the loitering Squad Pod, for it to descend to pick them up.

As soon as his boots hit the ground, he saw something half-buried in the dirt.

Picking it up, he saw that it was a snow globe, with a small crack in it. Inside was an image of the North Pole, with a building that said "Santa's Workshop" on it. On the bottom, someone had scrawled a note in dark ink. The letters were slightly smudged, but still legible: "Merry Christmas, see you when I join you in a year, love, Day."

Denig sighed and shoved the snow globe into a pocket. *Someone's back home's gonna have a shitty day when they find out about this.*

The Squad Pod arrived, and he jumped in, along with the rest of the First. Once all five of them were tucked into the pod, they headed farther east. They needed to take a look at the Dusters' landing zone.

Marine Corps Air Facility Schilt,
Near Jordan, Eastern Shapland

Major Terry Kawamura looked at the large monitor in front of him. They included reports that came in from Force Recon, as well as the data from the Navy ships in orbit.

His CO, the Head of Operations Colonel José Jiminez, looked over the lieutenant's shoulder. "That is a shit-ton of aliens."

Kawamura pointed at the section of the screen that included the report from Staff Sergeant Denig. "And they brought along some SUVs."

Jiminez snorted at Kawamura's joking reference to the Dusters now having tanks. It didn't warrant more, as the Dusters' new toys were no laughing matter.

Realizing his joke had fallen flat, Kawamura went back to his computer. "I think I've got me a plan of attack."

"Good. Hurry it up over to the 121st. Courtney's waiting for it."

"Okay, but—"

Kawamura hesitated, and so Jiminez prompted him. "But what, Major?"

"It's not a very good plan of attack."

"Mind telling me what's wrong with it, Marine?" Jiminez asked with a bit of menace.

"It needs about a hundred more Marines, Sir." Kawamura was not intimidated by the colonel's tone.

And Jiminez was grateful for that. He preferred his subordinates to be honest.

"Well, unless you have a squadron in your hip pocket, you're stuck with what we've got. We've been outnumbered before, and you know what? The Corps is still here."

"Yes, Sir." Kawamura did not say what he was thinking, which was that the Corps would still be "here" even if every Marine on Troy died—they'd just all be back on Earth and the other colonies. Wouldn't do the dead ones much good.

But he knew better than to say that out loud. Instead, he just said, "All right, I'm uploading it to the Hell Raisers."

☆

"All right, Hell Raisers," Lieutenant Colonel Henry A. Courtney, CO of Marine Attack Squadron 121, shouted as soon as he finished giving the mission order to his pilots, "the bug eaters of Force Recon found us some targets and Ops has given us a battle plan. Now let's get out there and raise some hell on their sorry asses!"

Flight helmet in one hand and comp in the other, Courtney sprinted for the exit. The other fifteen pilots of VMA 121 followed right on his heels.

Sixteen AV16C Kestrels were lined up, cockpits open, ground crew standing around their aircraft.

"Is she ready for me, Ike?" Courtney asked his crew chief, Staff Sergeant Isaac N. Fry.

"All lubed up, wide open, and waiting for ya, Sir," Fry answered with a wink. "It's all I could do to keep her from bucking. She's going to cream all over them Dusters when you get her there."

"I ought to transfer you to Army artillery, Ike," Courtney said, shoving his helmet into Fry's waiting hands so he could use both of his while he went over his pre-flight checklist. "They've got women over there. Then you could stop having wet dreams about killer aircraft."

"No thankee, Sir, I've seen them doggie dames. Half of 'em look like they got teeth behind the wrong set of lips."

"And the rest have razor blades down there, I guess. Right?"

"You must'a seen 'em, too, Boss."

"Must have," Courtney said, with most of his attention on his checklist.

"You could transfer me t' the VMO, ya know. They got splittails over there, too, Sir."

"Uh-huh. *Officer* splittails. Do you really think they'd go for a grease monkey like you?"

"Hell, ain't all a them dollies ossifers. Some's NCOs like me."

"They're probably too refined for you, Ike."

Fry snorted.

Satisfied that his Kestrel was fully armed with its six five-hundred-pound scatter-blast cluster bombs and 10,000 rounds of 30mm depleted uranium rounds for its Hades guns, fully fueled, and prepped for the mission, Courtney tucked his comp into its pocket in his flight vest and took his helmet back from Fry.

Settled, plugged in, and ready for launch, Courtney called his pilots on the squadron freq. "Hell Raisers, are you ready?"

Eight reports came in, seven from the other flight leaders, and one from 1st Lieutenant John Power, his wingman. Everybody was ready.

"Schilt Tower," he said on the ground control freq, "VMA 121 requests permission to launch."

"VMA 121, permission granted," the control tower replied. "No incoming to watch for. You are clear on ninety degrees."

"Let's go!" Courtney shouted into his squadron freq. He gave Fry a thumb's up, returned the salute his crew chief popped at him, then taxied for takeoff.

Two by two, the sixteen Kestrels flashed down the runway and launched into the sky. At two thousand meters altitude, some twenty kilometers east of the airfield, they shifted into four divisions and began to spread widely—when they reached their target, they'd be attacking along a fifty kilometer-wide front.

A Hundred and Fifty Kilometers East of MCAF Schilt

"Hell Raisers, Hell Raisers, I have the target on my forward-ground," Lieutenant Colonel Courtney called on his squadron freq.

A rapid-fire series of squelches and broken words told him that all of his pilots also saw the Duster formation on their ground-searching radars. The jerkily advancing aliens formed a rough rectangle about fifty kilometers wide and twenty deep.

"Full spread," Courtney said. "We'll hit them front to back with scatter-blasts, spin about, and hit them back to front with Hades. Acknowledge."

Another series of squelches and broken words told him everyone understood the order. A glance at his sideways radar showed him the sixteen aircraft spreading out online; they'd be three kilometers apart when they began their bombing run.

"Remember, their trip-A is dumb artillery. No seekers, so just watch out for objects to dodge." Courtney didn't really need to remind his squadron, they'd all been thoroughly briefed on the fire-and-forget anti-air artillery that had killed First Lieutenant Schilt. But a reminder never hurt, just in case it slipped someone's mind in the heat of battle.

While the Kestrels were spreading and Courtney was giving his reminder, they dropped from the two thousand meters at which they'd been flying to a hundred and fifty meters for their bombing and strafing runs.

They didn't see the thin picket line that led the mass of Dusters, but the pickets had seen them when they began dropping, and signaled the maneuver to their commanders.

The Duster AA artillery began firing just as the Kestrels began dropping their scatter-blasts. Not all of the alien guns were ready to fire, and none of them had the range yet. Most of the AA guns turned rearward, to fire at the aircraft once they passed. They still didn't have the range, and their shells were too high when they burst, showering their shrapnel harmlessly groundward.

Harmlessly to the humans, that is. The plummeting shrapnel added to the mayhem and murder flung out by the scatter-blasts' cluster bombs, ripping huge holes in the mass of Duster infantry that followed the AA guns.

VMA 121 flew twenty-five kilometers past the aliens' and spun about for its reverse run. Taking advantage of the small amount of time allowed by the maneuver, Courtney looked at his displays to make a quick damage assessment of the enemy formation.

He smiled grimly at what he saw, and muttered, "Take that, you sonsabitches." According to his displays, the squadron had damaged, destroyed, or killed about fifteen percent of the Dusters and their machines.

The Hell Raisers closed on the back of the formation, and their 30mm Hades guns began pouring destruction into the rear of the tanks, many of which exploded when the massive rounds slammed into their weapons lockers.

But this time, the triple-As had the range. Anti-aircraft artillery shells burst their deadly blossoms in a wall in front of the squadron.

"Break!" Courtney screamed into his comm, and jerked his Kestrel into a vertical climb. The aircraft staggered when chunks of hot metal thudded into its underside.

"Seven is hit!" First Lieutenant Wilma Hawkins shouted. "I'm going down." Then only static.

Courtney barely heard her. He was too busy trying to wrestle his wounded Kestrel under control.

"Ten—" was all Captain Robert Dunlap got out before his Kestrel exploded, showering heated chunks of itself into the air, and pelting the ground.

There were more reports of damage from other pilots. Courtney barely registered them as he cried, "C'mon" to his controls, trying to keep the Kestrel steady and rising.

Another volley of anti-air artillery flew into the sky and burst into murderous flowers. But it wasn't as effective as the first; the Dusters didn't have ranging radar for the guns, they all had to be manually aimed. Some of the shells went too high, but most burst too low to hit the rapidly climbing Kestrel. Still, some found targets.

Courtney's speed slowed as he climbed. He was almost down to stall speed by the time he reached three thousand meters. Then he flipped his nose over and made a turn to the right, gaining speed and cutting across the front of the triple-A rather than resuming his flight into its front.

"Hell Raisers, Hell Raisers," he radioed, "get the hell out of here. See me, do the same, go your best angle to get free." He was still wrestling with his aircraft but had it well enough under control that he was able to change its angle of descent and turn away from the Dusters' fire.

Once he was clear, he took stock of his squadron. His displays only showed eight aircraft other than his own still aloft. Had VMA 121 really lost nearly half its strength in—he glanced at his chronometer—less than fifteen seconds? Who was still up?

"Hell Raisers, report!" he snapped. The command was unnecessary, one display told him which aircraft were flying and which were missing from the sky. Reporting gave his pilots something to do other than concentrate on how bad their situations were.

All eight reported in smartly, though Captain Daniela Bruce's voice sounded ragged and raspy when she said, "Two, in."

"Form on me," Courtney said once he heard from all his remaining pilots. In little more than a minute, nine Kestrels were lined up, hovering ten kilometers behind the aliens who had done so much damage to the squadron.

"Keep your distance," Courtney ordered. "On my command, fire your Hades at them until you run out of ammunition. Then follow me home."

He paused a beat, then shouted: *"Fire!"*

The Hades guns fired rapidly. Even in hundred-round bursts, it took little more than a minute for the nine Kestrels to expend their remaining ammunition. Other than a few blasts from destroyed tanks, they couldn't tell how much additional damage they did to the enemy.

Hands gripped tightly on the controls as he nursed his wounded aircraft, Courtney led his surviving pilots in a wide arc around the formation. Some wobbled, and Captain Bruce's Kestrel trailed a great deal of smoke.

But they all made it back to Schilt.

The nine surviving ones, anyhow.

Marine Corps Air Facility Schilt,
Near Jordan, Eastern Shapland

Major Kawamura's board lit up with a communiqué from Navy Intelligence in orbit of Troy.

"Sir," he said to Colonel Jiminez once he read through the report, "according to our birds in orbit, VMA 121 reduced the strength of the Dusters moving toward Jordan by twenty percent from its original numbers. They also report that the enemy has slowed its westward advance by half."

Jiminez nodded. "And what damage did the Hell Raisers take?"

"Seven Kestrels and pilots gone, two Kestrels badly damaged, including Colonel Courtney's."

Again, Jiminez nodded. It could've been better, but it could've been worse, too. Still, the Hell Raisers were now at half-strength, and all they did was slow the Dusters down...

One Hundred Kilometers West of Firebase Gasson

Two flights of MH 15 Alphonse attack-transports from the 9th Infantry Division's Mobile Intelligence squadron, each escorted by a two-aircraft flight of AV 16C Kestrels from Navy Attack Squadron 43, touched down in an area of open woodland and disgorged their passengers. Sixty kilometers to the north, a second pair of Alphonses touched down, and their passengers scrambled off. The Kestrels then escorted the Alphonses east, to a safe distance, closer to Millerton and the 9th ID's base.

Then the Kestrels flew back to take up loitering positions five thousand meters above the Mobile Intel squads. They were too high to hear from the ground, high enough to resemble raptor-like avians gliding on thermals. And far enough away from the enemy to be able to see and escape any anti-air artillery thrown their way if they were identified for what they were—the pilots of VA 43 had been briefed on what happened to VMA 121, and were in no hurry to reenact their Marine counterparts' fate.

Navy intel had reported the Duster force heading toward Millerton, and the headquarters at Camp Puller reported them advancing along a forty-kilometer front. Rather than observe the aliens head-on as the Force Recon Marines had, the soldiers of first platoon of the 9th Mobile Intel Company were going to recon its flanks.

The soldiers were more heavily armed than the Marines of Force Recon over on Eastern Shapland had been. They also had different orders: kill stragglers, and take prisoners if possible.

First and second squads were accompanied by First Lieutenant Miller on the south of the anticipated Duster route. Master Sergeant Bronson was with third and fourth to the north.

The ten soldiers of first and second squads quickly assembled around Miller, who wasted no time on repeating the orders he'd given the platoon at Gasson. Instead, all he said was, "If you need air, the Kestrels are 'Halo,' you're 'Snare.' You know what to do. Get it done. I'm with second squad."

Sergeant First Class Levi B. Gaylord gave his platoon commander a curt nod, signaled his four men with another nod, and headed slightly east of north at a rapid pace. His men unhesitatingly followed. To their left, Miller and second squad went north on an equal tangent to increase the distance between them and first squad.

Gaylord went fast, but not so fast that he couldn't observe his surroundings. The major trees didn't form a solid canopy and allowed considerable sunlight to penetrate to the ground. While the undergrowth grew in profusion, most of it was barely knee-high, and therefore did not provide a solid ground cover. A multiplicity of game trails traced through it, many easily wide enough for the soldiers to traverse only periodically touching the growth on either side. Gaylord frequently looked at the ground when he was on the trails, watching for the tell-tale tracks of Duster feet. He didn't see any gouges that could have been left by the aliens' talons. What he did see was dimples left by the feet—hooves?—of what he suspected were native ungulates and smaller footprints of other local fauna. Here and there was a pug mark of what he presumed was a carnivore. The carnivores seemed to be solo animals; he thought they were highly unlikely to attack the five-man group.

In less than an hour, the squads closed to half a kilometer short of the anticipated flank of the Duster formation. They were most likely to intercept outlying flankers or stragglers here. They set up in an echelon right formation, facing west, twenty meters between men, with Gaylord in the middle. The soldiers seemed to blend into the ground cover. Their camouflaged wardress was different from the Marines'; it tricked the eye into not seeing details, and fuzzed the edges of shapes, making them effectively invisible to the human eye. (It was anybody's guess what they looked like to Duster eyes.) A kilometer to their west, Miller and second squad went to ground in the same formation.

Gaylord didn't send a signal to Miller to inform the platoon commander that he and his men were in position. They were in a comm blackout unless a squad got into trouble and needed help.

He checked his sensors. Nothing even as large as a middle-sized dog showed up on his motion detector. In infrared, he saw only small splotches, the signatures of avians flitting among the trees. The smeller, set to pick up the air-born molecules emitted by the alien enemy, showed nothing. As far as Gaylord's sensors could tell, the Mobile Intel squad was alone with the local fauna, just a bunch of small creatures that presented no threat to the humans.

After about a quarter of an hour, Gaylord began to hear noises from the northwest, the din of thousands of Duster voices shrieking out their caws. Listening carefully, he thought he could make out the rumble and clanking of mechanical noises under the caws. Looking to his left and his right, he said in a voice that wouldn't carry much more than twenty meters, "Look alert, flankers might come now. Pass it."

PFC Cassius Peck on his right and Corporal Charles Hopkins on his left each turned and bared their faces to him, and nodded to let him know they heard the order, then looked away to pass the word.

With the enemy entering auditory range, Gaylord checked his comp for the feed from orbit. It showed first squad's position, not from "seeing" the squad, but from noting the location of his info request. That made him smile; his signal was sent by tight beam, undetectable by anything not along its path—there was no way the Dusters could intercept his call to orbit. The feed from orbit rode his tight-beam signal back down, making it equally undetectable by anything not along its path.

The nearest point of the Duster mass—*formation* felt like a too-disciplined word to describe the aliens' manner of grouping—clustered half a kilometer north and just over a kilometer west, or about level with where second squad should be. Too far away for a single voice to carry, but the massed caws and shrieks of the thousands of voices were growing steadily louder.

The resolution of the feed wasn't sharp enough to show individual aliens, only groupings. However, the vehicles near the front edge did stand out. If this formation was arranged the same as the ones the Marines on Eastern Shapland had observed, these were the Dusters' anti-air artillery.

He stopped watching the low-res orbital feed, as it couldn't pinpoint any Duster flankers or scouts in the vicinity. He and his men would have to rely on their eyes and ears, and the sensors they carried.

Distant gunfire suddenly broke out to the west, from the direction second squad's position. Seconds later, Gaylord heard second squad's leader, Sergeant Grace, break comm silence.

"Halo Two, Halo Two," Grace called, "Snare Two needs you. Many bad guys closing on us from the west. Help us out here. Over." There was a buzz of static, then Grace called again. "We need it *now*, Halo!" An increasing volume of gunfire was clearly audible under Grace's voice.

He's alerting all of us, Gaylord thought. *That's why he didn't use a tight beam to call for air*. He wondered if third or fourth squad was also under attack—they were too far away for him to hear a firefight from their locations north of the enemy mass.

Second squad's firefight told Gaylord the aliens probably knew more humans were nearby, so he broke radio silence. "Look sharp," he said into his squad's short-range freq. "They might already be on their way to us."

As he said that, he heard the scream of Halo Two's Kestrels diving toward the ground, and the yammer of their cannons firing in support of second squad.

"Snare One, Snare One, this is Halo One." Lieutenant Herbert Jones's laconic voice came over Gaylord's tight beam. "We're coming down to mezzanine level, just in case you need us in a hurry."

"Appreciate it, Halo One," Gaylord replied.

In seconds, he started to hear the drone of a Kestrel losing altitude.

Sergeant James Elision, on the squad's right flank, suddenly broke his comm silence. "Movement on the right flank!"

Gaylord looked at his motion detector. At its extreme limit, he discerned movement through the forest, three hundred meters to the squad's right front. "Stand tight," he sent to his men. As open as the woodland was, it wasn't open enough for him to see that far. The Dusters, if it was the aliens, had to be barely in view from Elision's position. Was it close enough for the flank man to see what was making the movement?

He continued looking at the motion detector's display. One, two, three, more. Jerky movement. Not good. If it was the aliens, he should be able to hear their calls at that distance. Or were their flankers moving silently?

"Halo One, Snare One," he sent. "Azimuth, three-one-zero. Range, three hundred. Movement. Say hello for me. Over."

"Snare One, Halo One," Jones said. "Three-One-Zero. Three hundred from you. I see it. Hiya, fellas."

The Kestrel's steady drone abruptly turned to a scream as it heeled over and dove. It cannons began yammering, firing explosive rounds at the ground and whatever was there. Then the timber of its engine changed again, shrieking as it twisted out of its dive and clawed for altitude. Its sound dopplered away, and now the caws of Dusters came through, coming closer and closer, rapidly.

"Get ready!" Gaylord yelled into his comm.

Faster than humans could have covered the distance, Dusters began flicking through the trees, coming straight at the right side of the soldiers' thin line.

"Oh, shit!" Gaylord swore as he took aim at a charging, shrieking alien. *Whoa! There's too many of them; more than five men can fight off. Even with air support.* He pulled the trigger and would have been astonished at hitting his target had he been conscious of the fact that the Duster he shot was running straight instead of jinking and dodging side to side the way he'd always seen the aliens charge before. They were cawing and shrieking, the way he had always heard them on the attack.

Situational awareness told him that his men were firing at the Dusters; a change in the pitch of the Kestrel above them told him it was returning for another strafing run. His training and duty as a squad leader made his actions automatic. He was able to function without thinking about what he should do.

Which was good, because this was a situation that didn't particularly bear thinking about.

He toggled his comm's command freq and called HQ.

"Snare One is being overrun," he reported in with a calmness he didn't feel. "Snare One requires additional air support and immediate extraction. Over." He kept shooting while making the request for assistance, help that he knew wasn't particularly likely to arrive in time.

Line sights on target. Pull the trigger. Shift aim. Repeat.

To his front, beyond the nearest enemy soldiers, the Kestrel's Hades gun tore up the ground, shrapnel from those rounds ripping gory chunks of flesh from the aliens' bodies, spraying thin red blood.

Gaylord was vaguely aware of new sounds entering the firefight—distant thumps, followed by closer, overhead cracks.

Ominous cracks.

The cracks of anti-aircraft artillery rounds exploding in the air.

Hot chunks of metal casing scythed down, mostly but not always behind the charging alien soldiers, shredding limbs from tree trunks, thunking into the ground, slicing into Duster bodies. Some jagged, razor-sharp fragments landed closer. Gaylord didn't hear the scream from PFC Charles Bieger, on the squad's left flank, when a piece of shrapnel knifed down and severed his left arm.

Lieutenant Jones's voice didn't register on him when the Kestrel pilot called out, "I'm hit! I can't make it back."

He didn't notice the tremor in the ground when the Kestrel slammed into the earth a few hundred meters to his rear. He couldn't, not with three Dusters on him, their talons slashing him to ribbons.

More Navy Kestrels arrived soon thereafter, but by that time, all that the pilots could see was scorched earth and dead bodies.

The human bodies far outnumbered the Duster ones, and the survivors among the latter had moved on. The pilots searched in vain for survivors among their own forces amidst the burning grasslands and bloody corpses.

Returning to base, the Kestrels reported this engagement lost.

Headquarters, North American Union Forces,
office of the Commanding General
Near Millerton, Shapland

"Sir, it's General Noll," Captain William Upshur said, standing in the doorway of Lieutenant General Harold Bauer's office.

Bauer looked up from the reports from Force Recon and VMA 121 on their actions against the Dusters on Eastern Shapland—reports that told of anti-air artillery and armored vehicles, things the Dusters hadn't had before.

"Thanks, Bill." He picked up his comm. "General, what can I do for you?"

Major General Conrad Noll, ranking Army officer on the planet, spoke in a flat tone. "General, it's my unhappy duty to inform you that the platoon of Mobile Intel scouting the flanks of the western Duster formation appears to have been wiped out. As were the AV 16Cs that were providing them with cover."

Bauer momentarily closed his eyes. Four Navy Kestrels in addition to the seven Marine Kestrels that had already been killed in the east. The human air assets were taking a severe beating.

"My sincerest sympathies for the loss of your brave soldiers," he said. "Let your staff do their jobs. Your platoon will be avenged. As soon as possible, we will recover all the bodies. Bauer out."

After closing the connection, he looked at Upshur. "I want to conference all major element commanders in thirty minutes."

"Aye aye, Sir," Upshur said, and backed away to set up the conference call.

Thirty minutes later

"We're ready, Sir," Brigadier General David Porter said. The Chief of Staff stood next to a bank of eleven monitors that had been set up inside Bauer's office. The three major element commanders and their operations chiefs looked out of six of the monitors. Bauer's operations chief and the commanders of the three independent commands out of the other five.

"Thank you, gentlemen," Bauer said. "You've read the reports."

It wasn't a question. He knew they had to have read them; part of the reason for giving them half an hour's warning for the meeting was to make sure they had time to read them.

"The Dusters have weapons they haven't used before. We must change our tactics to meet this new threat." He looked at the commander of the 2nd Marine Air Wing and the commander of the Navy's Air Group Five (and highest-ranking Navy officer planetside). "General Bearss, Captain McNair, continue slowing the enemy advance and degrading their capabilities. Use stand-off weapons, avoid putting more of your aircraft in situations where they might be killed. Your primary target at this time is the anti-air artillery."

To the commanders of the 1st Marine Division and the Army's 104th Artillery Regiment, he said, "General Purvis, Colonel Ames, deploy your laser and conventional artillery to strike the enemy as soon as they are in range. Your primary targets are the armored vehicles—and anything in the way.

"Colonel Reid, Lieutenant Colonel Grant, I want Force Recon and Mobile Intel to gather intelligence to the rear of the enemy formations, see if they have bases or weapons/supply caches behind we can strike against.

"I don't think we can expect any assistance from Task Force 8 for the foreseeable future. Let's defeat these Dusters before 2nd Army arrives. As before, Brigadier General Shoup will coordinate. That is all."

Bauer nodded to Porter, who turned off the monitors.

"You sounded awful confident there, Sir," Porter said.

"Marines have been in tighter spots before. So has the Army. We won it in the past, and we'll do it again."

"Let's just hope they don't come up with air assets."

"Yes, let's."

Two hundred and fifty kilometers east of
Jordan, Eastern Shapland

First section, 1st Force Recon Platoon retrieved its Squad Pods after the mass of Dusters passed, but before the Kestrels of VMA 121 engaged the enemy, and headed east, toward the enemy's landing site, a scorched area many square kilometers wide.

The Pods touched down at four different locations, all four kilometers from the landing site, so each squad could approach from a different direction; first and third from its flanks, second from its rear, fourth straight on.

Staff Sergeant Denig had his squad spread out at twenty-meter intervals. The Marines advanced slowly, watching carefully for any booby traps the Dusters may have left in their wake. They didn't find any. Along the way, they didn't see any earth-born birds or insects. Neither did they see any native avians or flying insectoids.

A small part of Denig's mind wondered how the crops were pollinated without insects or birds about. But he was easily able to compartmentalize that curiosity to the back of his mind, leaving the front of his mind free to focus on watching for alien surprises. That ability to concentrate on the important stuff while not completely forgetting the unimportant stuff was why he was promoted to sergeant, or so he had been told.

That was one of two things that his then-CO, Colonel Hector Santiago-Colon, had told him during the promotion ceremony.

"When you're up in the officer ranks," the colonel had said while placing the three-stripe patch on his arm, "it's all about the big picture. And when you're down in the lower ranks, it's all about what's right in front of you and that's it. But when you're a sergeant, you gotta think of the big picture *and* the little picture all at the same time. You're the bridge between the Leathernecks on the ground and the officers back at HQ. And you've proven, time and again, J. Henry, that you can do that. So go do it."

The other thing Santiago-Colon said was a truly terrible joke: "With the promotion, you also get a transfer: three stripes, and you're out."

Denig didn't even like baseball.

Three kilometers in, Denig's squad reached cropland. The first was a field of half-grown corn, its stalks shoulder high. Six hundred meters farther, they encountered lower growing crops, stalky legumes of some sort. Beyond them, a farmstead was visible, near the center of the area in which the Dusters had landed. The scorched area began at what was now the far edge of the legume field. Denig stopped his squad there to observe.

From here, he could see that the scorching wasn't solid, but was overlapping spots where the alien landing craft had touched down. Here and there, where the ground wasn't blackened, were broken and trampled beanstalks. They watched for twenty minutes without seeing anything moving; not a person, not an alien, not a bird, not a grazing or hunting animal.

Looks like the animals that weren't killed by the Dusters landing got outta Dodge while the getting was good. Smart critters.

On Denig's signal, the squad rose and moved on, stepping carefully so as not to raise puffs of dust.

The Dusters had made no such attempt when they landed. The ground was scarred with lines and gouges from their talons, running helter-skelter, overlapping and obliterating each other so it was impossible to estimate how many there had been. There were also the very distinctive tracks of the tank-like anti-aircraft vehicles, running westward in straighter lines.

Denig stopped his squad less than a hundred meters from the farmstead, and the Marines went to ground. Corporal John

Rannahan faced the rear, watching for anyone approaching from that direction. They all used their motion detectors.

A whitewashed, two-story, gable-roofed structure with a wrap-around veranda was center-most: the farmhouse. To its right and slightly behind was a barn-like structure, likely a garage for farm vehicles and storage. An open-sided forge stood twenty meters to the side of the barn. Denig could hear the chugging of a generator shed, though his view of it was blocked by the barn. Fencing from what he thought was probably an animal enclosure jutted from the far side of the house, though Denig didn't hear any animal sounds from it. A silo stood twenty meters tall beyond it.

Denig turned his helmet's ears all the way up, listening for any sounds other than the muffled generator noise and breeze-ruffled leaves. He heard none. He studied the farm buildings and yard with his eyes. There was no movement save for vagrant leaves gusting with the breeze, and curtains fluttering in three second-floor windows of the house. He turned on his Sniffer to sniff for the telltale airborne organic chemicals of Duster scent. It was faint, but the aliens' scent was stronger than it should have been if it was only the residue of the Dusters that had already left.

But was it current, telling of Dusters present now? Or was it residual, from the passage of the thousands who had gone beneath them under the trees?

Slowly, cautiously, he turned about, aiming the Sniffer in a circle. He found a scent moving westward, in the direction of Jordan. But the strongest scent was clearly to his front—from the farm buildings.

He prepared a burst transmission tight beam to the Navy in orbit, to be relayed by tight beam back to the other squads, and to Force Recon headquarters at Camp Howard: *Dusters are here, but out of sight, numbers unknown.*

In little more than a minute, replies came from the other squads: *Same here.*

Then a two-word reply from Camp Howard: *Continue mission.*

They needed more intelligence, more information.

Denig tight-beamed another message: *First squad, sending two in close.*

Staff Sergeant Bordelon, third squad leader to the north of the complex, sent back, *Three sending two.*

Denig tapped Corporal Charles Brown on the shoulder, and the two rose to crouches and started toward the forge. At a hundred meters, their camouflage made them extremely difficult to focus on. Still, they continued to move in a crouch. They didn't know whether or not the enemy had detection devices set out, or what kind they might be, so they moved in random patterns. The two Marines didn't maintain a constant distance between themselves, but drifted closer then farther apart. Neither ever took more than three consecutive steps, nor did they have a rhythm to their paces; the pauses between their steps were irregularly spaced. And some steps were normal weight. Others were very soft. Their objective was to keep any audio nor seismic detectors from picking up anything that would read as the gait of a walking man.

It took them nearly half an hour to reach the open-sided forge. Brown watched the other buildings from outside the forge, while Denig, knife in hand, examined its interior. A quick look around showed nobody present.

Denig investigated farther. The gas-fired hearth was cold, and the gauge on the tank that fed it registered empty. Tongs, hammers, rasps, and other tools were scattered about. The anvil had been overturned. The oil in the quenching bucket had filmed over, with a few leaves and other bits of debris floated on top. Scuff marks on the dirt floor and stains on a hammer and tongs looked like the farmer, or whoever did the blacksmithing, had been attacked and put up a fight before being overwhelmed. Whatever happened here had happened long before this wave of Dusters had made planetfall.

Satisfied that he'd learned everything he could here, Denig signaled Brown, and the two continued to the barn, angling to circle around it, putting it between themselves and the house.

When they reached the rear of the barn, they could see a small shed, which was the source of the generator's chugging. A large gas drum squatted behind it. The drum had markings and symbols that weren't in any language or culture Denig was familiar with. He suspected it was something the aliens had brought with them. Had they known they would find a generator? Or had they brought their own?

Denig and Brown returned to the side of the barn. Some of the boards that formed its side were warped, and a number of them had been recently broken. Denig stood next to one of the larger breaks and listened carefully. When he didn't hear any sounds of occupancy, he risked looking through the break.

It was dim inside the barn. Other than diffused light, all the illumination was through slants from the breaks in the walls. Large machines were vaguely visible. Denig recognized a tractor, a small truck, a harvester, and a couple of farm carts for hauling produce. There were things he couldn't identify, either because they were blocked by other equipment or because they were too deep in the shadows.

He put his helmet next to Brown's and gave orders. Then they parted, Brown to the front left corner of the barn, and Denig back to the rear right corner. There they lay, observing the house. After twenty minutes without seeing any motion through the windows, Denig dropped to all fours and painfully made his way to the generator shack.

There were no warped boards on the sides of the shack, and none of the boards were broken, although several showed signs of recent repair. Denig crept around the shack and found a broken generator and gas tank on its other side. He would have liked to see inside the shack, but when he briefly checked he found its door locked. Still, the broken machine and tank beyond confirmed his thought that the Dusters had brought their own power supply. He wondered what they needed it for besides powering the house.

He returned to the rear corner of the barn and watched the house. On three occasions during the next half hour, he saw a long-jawed face looking through the parted curtains that covered windows on the second floor. He recorded each appearance for transmission to Camp Howard. The light inside was too dim for him to tell if they were the same face or different ones. And he didn't know whether NAU Forces Troy had enough facial recognition capability to distinguish among Duster faces. Without that, there was no way of knowing how many of the aliens had looked out the windows.

After watching long enough, he went back around to where Brown had been watching and gathered him to return to the rest of the squad. There, he tight-beamed his report to orbit for relay to Camp Howard. They waited for further orders.

Camp Zion, near Jordan

"KILO COMPANY, FORM UP!" GUNNERY SERGEANT JOHN L. YOUNKER ROARED, breaking the afternoon's quiet.

"Third platoon, up!" Staff Sergeant Douglas Haperman bellowed.

The camp became a riot of shouted voices, as the platoon sergeants, squad leaders, and fire team leaders yelled out, harrying their men into formation.

With a lot of yelling back and forth of, "What's up?" and jangling of equipment, the Marines of third platoon, Kilo Company, Third Battalion, First Marines scrambled into formation in front of their platoon sergeant. The other platoons of the company assembled to their sides. In less than a minute after Younker's command, all but a few stragglers were in company formation in front of him. Every one of them carried his weapons and ammo belt—it was a remote possibility, but if the camp got attacked so suddenly that they didn't have time to get to their bunkers, they wanted to be able to fight.

"*'Toon* sergeants, re-*port*!" Younker shouted.

The platoon sergeants had already gotten reports from their squad leaders, and about-faced to give their reports to Younker.

When it was his turn, Haperman stated loudly, "Third platoon, all present and accounted for!"

Younker turned to face the company's HQ bunker and waited.

Mere seconds passed before Captain Charles Ilgenfritz emerged, followed by the company's other officers.

Ilgenfritz came to attention two meters in front of Younker, who sharply saluted and said, "Sir, Kilo Company all present and accounted for."

Ilgenfritz returned the salute and said "Thank you, Gunnery Sergeant. Take your post."

"Aye aye, Sir." Younker turned sharply to his right and marched to his position in front of the leading edge of first platoon.

Ilgenfritz took a brief moment to look over his company. Not quite as big as it had been when it formed before leaving Earth, and some of the faces were still strangers to him—recent replacements for combat losses. But Kilo was a good company, capable of fulfilling any mission assigned to it.

And this one was a doozy.

"Marines," he said in a voice that carried clearly to every man in his command, "you know about the Duster force heading toward Jordan. Force Recon has located their landing site and discovered a force of unknown size still there. We are moving out in one hour. The landing site is our objective. Aircraft are on their way to transport us. When we reach our objective, we are to engage and destroy all enemy forces present there and destroy any and all weapons, munitions, and supplies present. If I receive any additional intelligence on what we can expect when we get there, you will be informed. When you are dismissed from this formation, your platoon sergeants will see to it that you have sufficient ammunition and other equipment and supplies for the mission."

Third Platoon's area, Camp Zion

"Squad leaders, with me," Staff Sergeant Haperman ordered as soon as the platoon reached its bunkers. The four gathered in front of him immediately. The rest of the men loitered where they could overhear. "We don't know what we're going to find out there. The Dusters might have left nothing more than a single team as fire watch. Or there could be a reinforced battalion. We just don't know. Even if Force Recon can't detect more than a fire team in the buildings, if there's any kind of underground structure, well, we all know that they use tunnels and caves.

"So, I want every rifle to have five hundred rounds and four grenades, minimum. Guns, four thousand each. Every fire team humps an extra ammo can for the guns. Yeah, that's an extra nine thousand rounds for the guns. If there's a lot of those buggers, that might not be enough. Let's hope it is enough. We can't rely on air support, the airedales might be needed to help out Regiment. And the squids topside have their own fight and might not be able to help us.

"Inspect your men. Make sure their weapons are clean, they've got their night-vision goggles, three days' rations, and plenty of water. Give me your reports when I get back with the extra ammo. Do it." He turned about and headed for the company's ammunition point to collect as many bullets and grenades as he could get.

"Whoa-shit, luna," Lance Corporal Daniel Inouye said, using the Hawai'ian word for "boss." "I don't like the sound of that one little bit."

"Yeah, 'little bit' is right. That's what you are, Danny, just a little bit chicken," Corporal John Capodanno replied.

PFC Jay R. Vargas laughed. "Little bit chickenshit!"

"I've been in enough shit with these bad bastards to have the right to be a little bit chicken, Jay." Inouye swung the flat of his hand at Vargas's head.

Vargas ducked out of the way and clucked.

PFC James K. Okubo watched the two from close to the entrance of the fire team's bunker. He was a last-minute addition to the team right before they left Earth, replacing PFC Christopher Nugent, whose wife had given birth to triplets. He was granted hardship leave, and Okubo was brought in to replace him fresh out of Boot.

"Knock off the grab-ass and line up so I can inspect your weapons," Capodanno ordered. Nobody grumbled. The inspection didn't take long, his men all kept their rifles and bayonets in good condition. Capodanno even checked their magazines to make sure there weren't any blockages.

Sergeant Alejandro Ruiz watched as his fire team leaders inspected their men, then ordered, "First squad, get everything you're supposed to take, then line up on me."

The twelve Marines of first squad scrambled to their bunkers and were back in two minutes with packs on their backs. Ruiz didn't bother inspecting the weapons and ammunition belts. He had full confidence in his fire team leaders. Instead, he inspected the contents of their packs. Nobody had more than four hundred rounds of ammunition, and not all of them had three days rations. He made a mental note of who needed how much of what. Water was a different problem.

Haperman was back in twenty minutes, accompanied by a Major Mite quarter-ton truck over-loaded with ammunition and rations. He had the squad leaders collect enough ammo and rations to bring their squads up to the requisite amount, including the extra cans of machine gun ammunition. Then he distributed the rest equally through the platoon. The riflemen now averaged six hundred rounds and five or six grenades each, there were five extra thousand-round ammo cans for the guns.

"You did good, Boss," Ruiz said *sotto voce* when he saw how much extra the platoon sergeant had brought back.

Haperman nodded and said equally quietly, "I wish we could take the vehicle with us." More loudly to the entire platoon, he said, "Now for water. Fall in." He marched them to the water point.

They heard the drone of approaching VSTOL P 53 Eagles.

In twenty minutes more, Kilo Company was aboard the Eagles, heading east, escorted by a division of four AT 5 Cobra ground attack aircraft. Their call sign was Chiricahua. The aircraft made a wide circle around the approaching Duster formation.

✪

After little more than an hour's flight, the Eagles touched down two kilometers from the farm buildings where Force Recon had confirmed Dusters were present. First platoon, with the company headquarters group, was to the east. Second and third platoons were north and south, respectively, of the building complex.

Captain Ilgenfritz checked his feed from orbit and noticed that the Force Recon squads weren't indicated. Which didn't surprise him at all; their uniforms were exceptionally good at avoiding detection throughout the entire range of the electronic and visual spectra.

Sergeant Timothy O'Donoghue, Ilgenfritz's communications officer, tight-beamed to orbit for relay to the FR squad leaders: "Leatherstocking, Leatherstocking. This is Chiricahua. Talk to me. Over."

As soon as the Force Recon squad leaders acknowledged that they were online, Bender nodded at Ilgenfritz, who turned on his relay comm.

"Chiricahua Six Actual. Update," Ilgenfritz said.

The four updates were brief, all variations on, "No change."

The Marines still didn't know whether they were up against a few aliens on fire watch, or a reinforced battalion.

"Leatherstocking, we are closing to five mikes. Will contact you again then. Chiricahua out." He issued orders for his platoons to advance to the edge of the scorched area. They went slowly, taking more than an hour to advance a kilometer and a half.

"Leatherstocking," Ilgenfritz sent when the company was in position. "Chiricahua Three is half a klick south of the built-ups. Can you send them a guide?"

A moment later, Staff Sergeant Denig sent back, "One Foxtrot Romeo on his way to your three."

"Chiricahua Three, Six Actual," Ilgenfritz said into his comm. "A guide is on his way to you. When he gets there, follow him and check out the buildings."

Denig didn't stutter-step his way to third platoon's location as he had when he first approached the buildings. If the Dusters had seismic sensors planted around the area, they already knew they were surrounded. He didn't rush, and reached third platoon twenty minutes after leaving the rest of his squad in place.

"Staff Sergeant Denig, 1st Force Recon," he reported when a sergeant escorted him to third platoon's commander. "I understand you're waiting for someone to show you the way through the barricades and deadfalls."

"Are there any?" Second Lieutenant Dan D. Schoonover asked.

"Not that we found. But you'll probably trip over my people if I don't stop you in time."

"Fair enough." Schoonover turned to Haperman. "In line. First squad, third, guns, second. I'm between first and third, you're with the guns. Line 'em up, and take Denig to Sergeant Ruiz so he can lead. Get online when we reach the Foxtrot Romeos."

"Aye aye." Haperman turned away, softly calling for the squad leaders so he could pass Schoonover's orders to them.

Battleship NAUS Durango,
in geosync orbit around Semi-Autonomous World Troy

Chief Intelligence Officer, Lieutenant Commander Finn McCleery, studied the data that had been sent up from Troy. Her job was to examine all the images taken by ships in orbit, by Marines and soldiers on the ground since the first Force Recon teams that investigated the invasion of Troy, and whatever else they were able to find on comps and other devices that had been left behind.

She noticed one major difference in the latest batch of images: the distinctive tracks made by the Dusters' new vehicles.

Her aide, Ensign Fred Zabitosky, stood behind her, peering at the screen over her shoulder.

"Looking for something to hang over your couch, Commander?"

"Nah, I'm partial to abstracts," McCleery said, a tinge of her Irish accent peeking through. When she first signed up, she had a full-on brogue, cultivated by growing up in South Boston, but a career in the NAU had reduced it to the occasional odd vowel.

Zabitosky peered more closely at the central image on her screen, which was the tracks left on the ground by the Duster vehicle. "I've never seen anything like that."

McCleery whirled on the ensign. "Say that again, Fred."

"Say what again?"

She glared at him. "Say. That. Again. Ensign."

"Yes, *Ma'am*." Zabitosky cleared his throat. "I've never seen anything like that, Ma'am."

She waved him off. "I don't give a shit about protocol, it's what you said. That you've never seen anything like this."

"Um, okay." Zabitosky was confused.

"Neither have I. And I've been spending the last week doing nothing but looking at evidence of the Dusters."

This just confused Zabitosky more. "Sorry?"

She touched a few controls on her comp, calling up a whole bunch of less familiar visuals. After a moment, Zabitosky realized these showed other worlds where they'd found wreckage that, they now knew, were the result of Duster invasions.

McCleery scrolled through: a world with four moons, a world with purple foliage, a world with massive (badly damaged) structures of crystalline design, a world where all the buildings were constructed on mountaintops, a world where the people lived in trees but nonetheless had impressive technology.

"What are you looking for, Commander?" Zabitosky asked.

But McCleery didn't answer, as she started scrolling faster and faster through the images.

Then she turned to Zabitosky. "Ensign, get Commander Yntema over here."

That got Zabitosky's attention, as McCleery never referred to anybody by rank unless someone who outranked her was in the room—or it was really important.

"Aye aye, Ma'am," Zabitosky said.

Five minutes later, the Durango's executive officer, Gordon Yntema, entered.

"I was just on my way to the mess, Commander, and today's the last of the real eggs. I'm potentially missing my last omelet, so this better be good."

"They make awful omelets in the mess, Sir," McCleery said with a small smile, "and I think this is something worth mentioning."

"What's that?" Yntema folded his arms and waited for the intelligence officer to impress him.

"I've been looking at the damage the Dusters did to the other seventeen worlds where they seemed to have wiped out all life. And there's an obvious pattern to all of it."

"We already knew that, Commander, and I've got an omelet waiting."

Holding up one finger, McCleery said, "Hold on, Sir, I'm getting there. Now, everywhere we've got the same style of damage: chaotic, thorough. All the destruction is either minor single-impact—probably from ships landing—or from weapons fire at ground level. The damage is from the bottom up. There's also the Dusters' tracks. Not all the locations have the type of ground that shows tracks, but the ones that do match what we've seen on the ground here on Troy after the Dusters come through: back-and-forth tracks with their talons."

"Commander—"

"Here's the thing," McCleery said quickly, "you know what I see *no* evidence of on *any* of the other seventeen worlds?"

"You really think it's a good idea to keep me in suspense, Lieutenant Commander?"

McCleery winced, the use of her full rank reminding her that she needed to get to the point. "Sorry, Sir, but I needed to set this up properly." She touched controls and showed once again the image of the unique Duster tank tracks.

"The wheels on the Duster tank have a very distinctive tread. And it's *deep*, too—even the worlds where you can't make out Duster footprints, you'd be able to see evidence of the tanks. If not the tread, at least the damage they've done from running over things. But aside from here on Troy—and that only in the last couple of days—there's been *no* evidence of this."

Yntema just stared at the screen, his brow furrowed, for several seconds.

Finally, McCleery broke the silence. "Worth losing out on an omelet?"

The commander waved that off. "The cook'll hold my omelet for me, lest he get my foot in his ass. I was just busting your chops. But this—" He let out a long breath. "This is—what is this? In your opinion, Commander?"

McCleery blew out a breath through her teeth.

"One of the things they teach us in spook school, Sir, is that the discrepant part of a set is the most noteworthy. Troy is now a discrepant part of the set of the Duster invasions. We know of eighteen invasions they've engaged in, and this is the first time they've felt the need to whip out the SUV of doom they've got down there."

"And what are we supposed to do with that information?"

Unable to help herself, McCleery grinned. "That's not for me to say, Sir. My job is to provide the intel. It's the job of you and those above to you to decide what to do with it. But it is my considered opinion that NAU forces have given the Dusters more of a fight than they've ever gotten before. Which may mean they're desperate."

"Or it may mean that they love that they're getting a real challenge for a change." He put a hand on McCleery's shoulder. "Good catch, Finn. I'll bring this to the captain, and we'll take it to the rear admiral. Meanwhile, I want a *full* write-up on this."

"Aye aye, Sir, with twenty-seven eight-by-ten color glossy photographs and four-part harmony."

"Say again, Commander?" Yntema asked with a quizzical expression.

"Old folk song, Sir, sorry," McCleery said sheepishly. She pointedly did not add that it was about someone who avoided the draft in the late 20th century back on Earth.

"You may need to give that spiel to the captain, Admiral Avery, or any number of other brass—try to keep it shorter next time."

Nodding, McCleery said, "Aye aye, Sir."

"Good work, Commander."

Firebase Westermark, Eastern Shapland

Staff Sergeant William Zuiderveld had just returned to the motion detector station with his coffee, which he put down as quick as he could in the console's cup holder.

"Damn, that's hot," Zuiderveld muttered. "We can fly through space, we can go to other worlds, we can terraform planets, but we haven't figured out how to make a cup that doesn't burn your fingers when you put hot coffee into it."

"It's a mystery, Sarge," Corporal Victoria Vifquain said from the station next to his. "I don't know how you can drink that sludge, myself."

"I'm a traditionalist, Vic. I pour it down my gullet."

Vifquain snorted. "I wouldn't use that stuff to polish my weapon—it might eat through the metal."

"Not a coffee fan?"

Laughing, Vifquain said, "Oh, I *love* coffee. That's why I can't drink *that*. Back home, I buy unroasted Kona beans, roast them myself in my big-ass roaster, and grind them in my burr grinder. *That's* coffee. *This*," she pointed at Zuiderveld's cup, "is industrial waste."

Shaking his head, Zuiderveld took a sip of his coffee—

—and just as he did, an alarm went off.

"Picking up motion, ten klicks northeast."

Vifquain checked her readout next to him. "Confirmed, ten klicks, bearing— What the hell?"

Having heard the alarm, their CO, Captain Michael Crescenz, came over. "What've we got?"

"Movement, Sir," Zuiderveld said. "Ten klicks northeast."

"Not our people?" Crescenz asked his personnel officer, Sergeant Robert Modrzejewski.

The sergeant peered at the readouts on Zuiderveld's board. "We don't have that many people in one place, Cap. So unless the 104th, the 1st Marines, *and* the Leathernecks decided to have a marching party—"

"Got it," Crescenz said. "So they're Dusters. Heading?"

Vifquain said, "Sideways, Cap'n."

That was not the answer Crescenz was expecting, as he figured the aliens would be bearing right down on them. "Explain, Corporal."

"I swear to you, Cap'n, when I realized what heading they're on, I got flashbacks. My brothers and I used to play war games when we were kids. What the Dusters are doin' reminds me of when we used to do medieval games and someone decided to do a siege of a castle."

Zuiderveld looked over at Crescenz. "Sir, I've been running some numbers while Corporal Vifquain was telling her bedtime story." That last part was said with a look at the corporal, who had the decency to look a bit abashed. "And she's right—they're moving in an oval, like they're gonna surround."

"Can C&C take them out?" Crescenz asked Zuiderveld.

The staff sergeant shook his head. "No, Sir, too close."

"Dammit, we need the 104th to engage," Crescenz said.

Modrzejewski consulted his tablet. "They're way out of position. We were expecting something more direct."

"Who's closest?"

"Lieutenant Albanese's platoon is nearby—in fact, they've been reporting movement, which is probably what we're looking at here."

"All right, let's take this up the ladder." Crescenz pointed at Zuiderveld. "Updates every five, copy?"

"Yes, Sir," Zuiderveld and Vifquain said simultaneously.

While keeping a sharp eye on his readout, Zuiderveld asked Vifquain, "These brothers you played war games with—these are the same ones that washed out of Basic, right?"

Grinning, Vifquain said, "Yup."

"How often did they win?"

Vifquain shrugged. "Never."

"Really?"

"Well, okay, there was the time I let Alberto win because it was his birthday."

Zuiderveld snorted. "Figures." Then he peered more closely at the readout. "Raises the question, though..."

"What question?" Vifquain asked.

"Well, last time I checked, this wasn't a medieval castle, and the Dusters weren't knights in shining armor. So why the fuck are they setting up a siege?"

Outskirts of Eastern Shapland

After receiving instructions through his headset comms, 1st Lieutenant Lewis Albanese turned to face the sergeants in charge of the fire teams in the fifth platoon of the 104th Artillery Regiment.

"We gonna see some action, Lulu?" asked Sergeant Michael Estocin of Fire Team One.

Albanese had reluctantly gotten used to that nickname, which he'd acquired when he got promoted to second lieutenant and had kept on elevation to first lieutenant, as the merging of the abbreviations for his rank and first name proved impossible to resist. He didn't mind overmuch because the alternative was for people to refer to him by his last name, which *everyone* mispronounced "al-ban-EES," rather than the proper "al-ban-AY-zee."

Answering Estocin's question, Albanese said, "Maybe yes, maybe no. HQ finally admitted that the Dusters're out there like we told them half-an-hour ago. Problem is, now we know why we ain't seen 'em yet—they're goin' around."

"Around what?" asked Fire Team Two's commander, Sergeant Leo Thorsness.

"The firebase."

"Takin' the scenic route?" Estocin queried.

Sergeant Dale Wayrynen, who commanded Fire Team Three, said, "Wait, what about all those booby traps we laid down?"

With a sigh, Albanese said, "It was good practice, but it ain't gonna do us much good if they're not coming at us."

The fifth had spent the entire morning laying down booby traps in preparation for the frontal assault that they were expecting. Now the brass wanted them to scout the Dusters, see what they were actually doing, but not to engage.

Which was fine with Albanese. He only had half a dozen fire teams out here. There was a whole fucking regiment of Dusters—they'd have their asses handed to them.

Then a thought niggled at the back of the lieutenant's mind. "Leo, I need the trap map."

Thorsness nodded and then cried out to the soldiers under his command who were in ready positions amidst the trees. "Corporal Fleek, front and center!"

The soldier in charge of keeping track of all the booby traps they'd laid, Corporal Charles Fleek, got up from underneath a bush and ran toward the sergeant. "Sir!"

Thorsness held out a hand and said, "Tablet, Corporal."

"Yes, Sir." Fleek pulled out a tablet from his pack and handed it to the sergeant.

Taking the tablet from Fleek, he said, "Thank you," and then activated it and handed it to Albanese.

After two seconds of looking at the layout of where they'd put the traps, the lieutenant muttered his grandmother's favorite curse, *"Faccim."*

"What's up, Lulu?" Thorsness asked.

Rather than answer directly, Albanese activated his comms. "Westermark, fifth, Westermark, fifth."

"Fifth, Westermark."

"Westermark, this is Lieutenant Albanese. We've got Dusters heading right toward one of our claymores. Estimate they kick it in twenty minutes."

There was a brief pause. "Say again, Lieutenant."

"I say again, the Dusters are going to set off one of our claymores in twenty minutes. Please advise."

Another pause, then another voice came on, which Albanese recognized as belonging to Colonel Adelbert Ames. "Lieutenant, this is Colonel Ames. Can you retreat without engaging the enemy?"

Because it was a bird colonel on the other end, Albanese didn't say what he wanted to say, which was *only if the enemy is blind and stupid, and we both know they're neither.* Instead, he blew out a breath and said, "Exceedingly unlikely, Sir."

Yet another pause. "Lieutenant, you are hereby ordered to prepare to engage the enemy, should they trip the claymore and engage you. Try to minimize casualties." It was to Ames's credit that he could obviously tell that last sentence sounded ridiculous even as he said it, but he had to give the order.

"Yes, *Sir.*"

"Give 'em hell, soldier."

"We absolutely will, Colonel. fifth out."

Albanese paused for one moment to cross himself and then turned his comms to address all the soldiers in the fifth.

"People, we've got Dusters about to get blown to hell by those claymores we laid down this morning over at grid 7B. They're probably gonna be a little cranky, so we're gonna need to calm them down a bit. Take positions—we do *not* engage until they do."

He paused and thought about the fact that he was likely never to eat his grandmother's pasta and sauce ever again. That pissed him off and made him even more determined to take down as many of them as he could.

"And if they do—*when* they do—we'll let 'em know that they fought the fifth!"

Firebase Westermark, Eastern Shapland

Colonel Ames listened to the reports coming in from the comms of all the members of fifth platoon.

He heard nothing until the claymores went off. It was to Lieutenant Albanese's credit that they didn't make a sound until they had to.

He heard the screams of the wounded Dusters and the noise as they jinked their way toward the fifth.

He heard the report of weapons fire from Army guns, as well as the return fire from the Dusters.

He heard the screams of the human wounded and the Duster wounded. There were far too many of the former and not enough of the latter.

When he heard nothing but the Dusters continuing on their merry way from the few comms that were still intact after the engagement, Ames quietly saluted to the air in front of him.

"We'll get them for you, Lieutenant, that's for goddamn sure." Then he turned to the comms officer. "Get me General Bauer, *now*."

"Yes, *Sir*."

Battleship NAUS Durango,
in geosync orbit around Semi-Autonomous World Troy

Captain Harry M.P. Huse felt Headache #4 coming on.

Ever since he'd taken command of *Durango*, Huse had started classifying his headaches. Number one usually came on when he had to deal with the brass, and was the one that felt like a needle was being driven through the bridge of his nose, while #2 was the throbbing at his temples that generally accompanied an argument with his husband. He hadn't had #3 in years—that ache in his forehead only showed when he had to bring an underling up on charges, and he hadn't had any underlings that fucked up in either of his last two postings. The *Durango* crew, in particular, had been exemplary, even now against as brutal an enemy as the human race had ever faced.

As for #4, that was a sharp pain behind the eyes that characterized reading a report he didn't like.

This particular report was from his chief intel officer, Lieutenant Commander McCleery, which stated that this was the first time in eighteen engagements that the Dusters had utilized tanks, as there was no evidence of any kind of large ground vehicle on the other seventeen worlds.

Huse was reading her report in advance of the lieutenant commander herself reporting along with his XO, Commander Yntema.

Just as he got to the end of it, the comms rang out with the voice of his adjutant, Lieutenant Rufus King Jr. "Sir, the XO and CIO are here, as ordered."

"Send 'em in."

The two officers entered.

Huse waved his right hand in the direction of the guest chair. He was grateful that Navy tradition was that you only saluted a senior officer once per day, and then only in duty areas. You didn't salute inside. Of course, a spaceship was entirely inside, but for these purposes, an office counted as inside. For his part, Huse didn't even like the daily saluting, and in fact, he'd been written up more than once for violating protocol by not saluting properly or at all. Everyone on *Durango* knew the hierarchy, and as long as they paid attention to their superiors, Huse didn't give a shit if they put their hands to their foreheads. It was like an oath of office: you only needed to swear it the once.

Yntema and McCleery sat down in the guest chairs, as requested.

"Sir," Yntema said, "I'm afraid Commander McCleery has a new report."

"I don't need another headache, Gordon."

"None of us do, Sir, but we've got one."

Huse looked at the intel officer. "Go ahead."

McCleery cleared her throat, glanced at Yntema, who nodded, and then said, "Sir, we've got confirmation that the Dusters are taking positions surrounding Firebases Westermark, Gasson, and Cart."

"Surrounding?"

"Yes, Sir."

"All the way around?"

"Yes, Sir."

Huse frowned. "On purpose?"

"Looks like, Sir," McCleery said. "They've moved into position completely surrounding each firebase."

Calling the report up on his screen, Huse stared at the report, which showed the images they'd taken from orbit.

"I'm not buying it," Huse finally said.

"Sir?" McCleery asked, confused.

"Oh, I believe your report," the captain said quickly. "But I'm not buying that the Dusters are this stupid. They've been tactically sound up until now. Why suddenly go all stupid on us?"

McCleery said, "If I may, Sir?"

Huse made a *go-ahead* gesture.

"This may relate to my original report about the ground vehicles. This may be new territory for them. After all, this is the first time in eighteen engagements that they've had to whip out the big guns. Maybe they're in tactically unfamiliar territory."

"Maybe." Huse stared at the report some more.

Then he got to his feet. The two junior officers did likewise.

"Either way, we gotta run this up the ladder so they can run it down to the surface. But we can't just assume the enemy is stupid. Nobody ever won a war assuming that." Then he smiled. "Of course, lots of people have won wars *because* the enemy is stupid. But that's for the enemy to deal with. We just need to fight them."

"Yes, Sir."

"Rufus!"

King stuck his head into Huse's office. "Sir?"

"Tell Admiral Avery I need to talk to him ASAP."

"Yes, Sir."

"You two are dismissed. Reports every fifteen from intel."

"Aye-aye, *Sir*," McCleery said.

A few minutes later, after Yntema and McCleery had returned to their stations, King made a slight yelping sound.

Frowning, Huse got up and went to the doorway to his office, only to see King standing at attention and Admiral Avery himself approaching.

"At ease, Lieutenant," Avery said.

King shifted to parade rest.

"Sir, I would've come to you," Huse said.

"I need to stretch my legs," Avery said. "What's the scoop?"

They both entered the office, and Huse filled him in on both reports he'd gotten from McCleery.

"We've been getting reports from the ground that indicate the same thing—good to get confirmation up here." Avery rubbed his jaw. "Interesting about the ground vehicles, but I don't see that that matters much in the here and now."

"Agreed, Sir, but it does show a pattern, as intel indicated. The Dusters may be in uncharted waters."

"That just may mean they'll fight harder. Then again, surrounding our Marines and soldiers down there may mean the same thing."

"Yes, Sir."

Avery got up from the guest chair and said, "Good work, Harry."

Huse rose and nodded. "Thank you, Admiral."

Turning toward the door, Avery said, "Tell King to contact Davis and have him be ready to send a squib to the surface."

"Aye-aye, Sir."

Camp Zion, Near Jordan, Western Shapland

"Say what?" Corporal John Mackie yelped when he heard the Navy intelligence report. "Are they out of their ever-loving minds?"

"They're aliens, Mackie," Sergeant James Martin, his squad leader, said patiently. "Who knows what goes on in their minds? I sure don't. And if anybody higher-higher knows, they aren't telling me."

Mackie shook his head and looked at the men in his fire team. They were staring at him and Martin as though the two were crazy. Or at least like the Navy intel report was.

"We're Marines," Martin said. "When we're surrounded, all that means is we get to shoot in all directions." He left, headed for the platoon CP bunker. He hadn't said it, but he agreed with Mackie; the aliens had to be out of their fucking minds.

Mackie glared at his men. "You heard Sergeant Martin," he said. "All this means is we get to shoot in all directions." He shook his head in disgust. "Crazy fucking aliens," he muttered.

Lance Corporal Cafferata shook his head as he checked his weapon. "That's just nuts. I mean, completely surrounding a defensive position like that, they're all set up for a circular firing squad."

"Not if they hit us in front of them instead of their own people behind us," Orndoff said.

Horton shrugged. "We can duck."

"Damn right." Cafferata laughed and slapped the new PFC on the back. "Then we come up shooting. Got nowhere else to go, anyhow, since we're surrounded, so we fight those Dusters even harder."

"All right, people, let's get ready to rumble," Mackie said. "Sound off, 3/1/3."

"Here," Cafferata said.

"Present," said Ordnoff.

Horton just said, "Yo."

"Let's move out."

As they marched to position, Horton muttered to Ordnoff, "You know what I don't get?"

"Probably a lot," Ordnoff said.

Horton snorted. "Don't the Dusters realize that we set up the firebases to have mutually supporting fire? We should be able to hit the ones around Gasson from behind from Cart and Westermark."

"Pretty sure that's why Mackie said, 'fucking aliens'," Ordnoff said.

"Can the whispering," Mackie said. "Double time! Horton, take point."

They moved toward the firebase, having to reposition themselves because they were prepared for a frontal assault, not a weird-ass siege.

Horton was still the rookie in the squad, so he took point. He moved to take cover in one tree, then Ordnoff moved ahead while Horton covered him, then Cafferata moved past them both while they covered him, with Mackie the last to progress from the squad.

Each squad moved in the same formation, taking cover behind trees or rocks or bushes, depending on what the terrain presented.

For some reason, Horton's mind went to his best friend, Fred Phisterer. They had grown up together in Regina, Saskatchewan, living next door to each other. They went to school together, enlisted together, went through Boot Camp together.

But once they survived Boot, they got assigned to different units. Fred was sent off to a base in Europe, specifically an airbase in Budapest.

Horton got assigned to India Company, which got sent to this godforsaken planet that had been overrun by aliens who had really dumb strategies.

"Whatcha gonna do?" Horton had said when Fred apologized for his billet. "We dance where they tell us. No big deal."

"Send me a postcard from Troy," was the last thing Fred had said to him.

The last thing he'd said back was, "The mail don't come that far."

Mackie having moved to the front, it was back to Horton, who went past his squadmates and took point once again.

As he did so, something caught Horton's eye as he once again moved forward, taking point.

Holding up a fist, he stopped moving, and then looked down.

Activating his local comms for the squad, he said, "Tripwire."

Mackie nodded. "3/1/3, hold position. Horton, check it out."

Shouldering his rifle around to his back, Horton knelt down and examined the tripwire.

Slowly moving to his left, he tracked it visually, being careful not to touch anything, finally finding a small device.

"Whatcha got, Horton?" Mackie asked.

"Could be a paperweight for all I could tell you, Corporal, but I'd bet real money that it's an explosive."

Mackie immediately activated company comms. "India Company, be advised, 3/1/3 found a booby trap, repeat, 3/1/3 found a booby trap. Eyes wide, everyone."

All the other squads acknowledged in short order.

Then a voice screamed, "Shit!"

"Back off, back—"

An explosion shook the ground, and everyone stood at the ready with their rifles.

Voices screamed over comms.

"Gaienne's down!"

"Burnes, move!"

"Corpsman!"

Sergeant Martin's voice bigfooted everyone. "3/2/1 down. Tripwire tripped. Everyone, stay frosty, we're gonna be up to our ass in Dusters in a minute."

"Confirm, Top," came the voice of Corporal Mausert. "We got movement bearing right on us."

"This is it, India Company," Martin said. "Stay frosty. *Oo-rah!*"

Around Horton, everyone cried out, "*Oo-*rah," but Horton himself couldn't bring himself to say it.

He'd only been with the squad a short time, having replaced PFC Zion. He wanted to fit in with the other guys, to become part of the group, but he didn't quite feel like he'd earned his place.

At least I found the tripwire, he thought as he aimed his weapon, waiting for the Dusters to come in sight.

"Here they come!"

Horton heard them first, the sound of several dozen Dusters jinking back and forth, the dirt and brush being kicked up by their movement.

And then they broke through, firing away.

Taking aim, Horton shot at them from behind his tree.

At that point, training took over. There were no thoughts of fitting in with the squad, of filling Zion's shoes, of his family back in Regina, or of Fred Phisterer.

No, all he thought about now was the imperative of shooting Dusters and not getting shot by them.

His weapon became an extension of his own arm at that point. Aim, shoot; aim, shoot.

Three Dusters went down from his weapons fire, and three more were obviously wounded.

Aim, shoot.

He heard a scream behind him that sounded a lot like Ordnoff, but he wouldn't take his eye off the Dusters, as more of them were coming, and he had to keep shooting.

A dozen of them were headed right for him. There had been two score of them, but the other eighteen were taken down, but those dozen kept coming, and Horton was out of ammo.

Shit.

The Dusters kept firing. Horton huddled behind the tree to reload his weapon, hyperaware that the enemy drew closer each second it took.

He also saw that Ordnoff wasn't the only one who went down; he was just the only one who had time to scream. Mackie, Cafferata, and Ordnoff were all bleeding on the ground, and it didn't look like any of them were breathing.

His weapon reloaded, he fired at much closer range now, but to much less effect.

Aim, shoot.

Pain sliced through his bicep as one of the Dusters' weapons got his arm.

Eyes tearing, he blinked them away and kept firing.

Aim, shoot.

They were almost on top of him now, and he couldn't take them all out himself.

Or could he?

Looking down him, he saw the tripwire that he'd spotted, the very booby trap that the Dusters had so poorly lain for them. There were a mess of them, but only one went off.

Anyone for two?

The Dusters were almost on top of him now, and there was no way he was going to survive.

So he kicked the tripwire.

The world exploded, and Horton's last thought was he was glad Fred, at least, would survive. He did regret never sending that postcard...

Firebase Gasson, Shapland

Captain Patricia Pentzer bellowed to her gunners, "I need firing solutions, people!"

First Lieutenant Abram P. Haring reported from Gun 1, "Dusters are blocking the ground vehicle headed for us, but we've got a shot on the Dusters themselves that are closing in on Cart."

"Do it," Pentzer said. Since the Dusters were being kind enough to surround the firebases, Pentzer was happy to take whatever target presented itself.

From Gun 2, First Lieutenant William H. Newman reported, "We've got our own people blocking some of the shots on Westermark, but we've got a clear shot on the vehicle."

"Take it."

For her part, Pentzer watched as the battle unfolded, and her jaw dropped.

"Jesus," she muttered.

"What is it, Cap?" Sergeant Norton asked.

"The Dusters are taking shots without *any* regard to what they're hitting. They're taking out their own people as well as ours."

Norton shuddered as he peered over her shoulder at the display. "Takin' out a lot more of ours, though."

"Fire," Newman said.

His assistant gunnery captain, Master Sergeant David Ayers, said, "Charging," activating the laser battery, double-checking that it was aimed at the Dusters' ground vehicle, and once the indicator showed green, he fired.

The lasers weren't visible to the naked eye, but the heads-up display showed the arc of the beam in infra-red as it issued forth from the very large gun, right at its intended target.

The beam from Gun 2 was absorbed by the Duster vehicle, with absolutely no indication of any harm to the enemy target. No temperature changes, no dislocation of the metal surface, nothing.

"No damage," Ayers said, "say again, *no* damage."

"Shit," Newman said. "Fire again."

"Charging." Once again, Ayers went through the motions, and the weapon fired again, but nothing happened.

"Still no damage, LT."

Newman shook his head. "Hell with it, no point wasting good energy after bad. Switch to the Dusters themselves. Maybe we can clear a path."

Meanwhile, Gun 1 was already doing what Newman had realized was his best course of action.

"A dozen Dusters down," Master Sergeant Henry Fox said to Haring after Gun 1 fired upon the Dusters.

"Band-aid on a bullet wound," Haring muttered.

"Sir?"

"Just keep firing, Sergeant."

Pentzer was watching her own HUD when she saw the ground vehicle that was approaching their own firebase shot a wide-beam laser that was actually visible to the naked eye.

"Oh, Jesus," she muttered as the beam sliced through a dozen Marines, several pieces of artillery, and all the way through to the Dusters on the other side of the firebase.

The beam from the vehicle vaporized everything in its path.

"What the hell's wrong with them," Fox cried out, "they're taking out their own!"

"Yeah, we know, Sarge," Pentzer said, "but they're taking out ours, too. Keep firing on the support, and somebody get on the horn to Colonel Ames and tell him to get everyone the hell *out* of the line of fire of those tanks!"

Firebase Cart

Sergeant William Pelham lobbed three grenades at the ground vehicle, all of which exploded harmlessly as it lumbered toward him and his Marines.

"Keep firing!" he cried out unnecessarily.

On either side of him were the two Corporal Greenes. Corporal John Greene fired his automatic rifle on continuous burst on the tank, while Corporal Oliver Greene went with explosive bursts on the Dusters themselves.

Only the latter was having any luck.

As soon as Pelham had both of them assigned to his squad, he knew that it was going to be a problem, especially since both corporals were dark-skinned with shaved heads and no facial hair. They were both within an inch of each other in height. They were not related.

No nickname stuck, so he finally just started calling them by first name. Even when he included rank, it was "Corporal John" and "Corporal Oliver."

"What the hell's that thing made of?" John asked as his weapons fire proved utterly ineffective.

"Fucked if I know, Corporal John, but keep firing." Pelham tossed another grenade. "Fire in the hole!"

The grenade did no more good than John's weapons fire.

"Wanna gimme a hand with these Dusters, Boss?" Oliver asked.

"That tank ain't stopping," John added.

Pelham sighed. "All right, fine. I was hoping if we kept hitting the wall enough times, sooner or later it'd crack, but that wall's tough and we ain't got that kinda time. Let's—"

The front of the tank then started to glow red.

"Shit, it's armed!" John said, even as he turned his weapons on the Dusters who were jinking back and forth toward them on the right-hand side of the tank.

"Hit the deck!" Pelham cried out.

But even as all three went down on the ground, the world suddenly got *extremely* hot.

Pelham and both Corporal Greenes didn't feel anything after that, and neither did anyone else in their platoon.

Elsewhere, Corporal Joseph Frantz was bellowing to his people, whether they outranked him or were subordinate to him, "Hit the sides! Stay away from that damn beam!"

Everyone started to get out of the way of the ground vehicles, instead going for the sides, where the Dusters were jinking back and forth and moving alongside their new toy.

Then the beam fired again, in the same direction—but there was nobody and nothing there.

Private First Class Henry Du Pont said to Frantz, "Hey, did they just fire at nothing?"

"Not just that, but that tank on steroids hasn't changed course, even after we got out of its way."

"Ain't there a saying about gift horses and mouths?" Du Pont asked.

Frantz snorted. "I grew up with horses, Private, and all's I can tell you is that horses have really bad breath. Either way, I ain't stickin' my head in one. Let's keep at it!"

Firebase Westermark

Captain Michael Crescenz saluted Colonel Adelbert Ames, the CO of the 104th as he approached.

"Report," Ames said, returning the salute.

Crescenz returned to parade rest and said, "Sir, those tanks of the Dusters are killers. But they're all front-firing, Sir. We've got to rearrange the troops so they're attacking from the side."

"That's where most of the Dusters are anyhow, aren't they, Captain?"

"Yes, Sir."

Ames nodded. "We need to take those vehicles out."

"Sir, none of the laser batteries have made a dent."

"Dammit."

"Captain Pentzer used stronger language, Sir."

"I'll bet she did. What are we looking at for casualties?"

"We're down thirty percent, Sir, and that's just KIA. Lot more wounded, but they're still fighting as best they can."

"And the enemy?"

Crescenz was reluctant to answer, and he hesitated.

"Out with it, man," Ames snapped.

"Ten percent, Sir. And that's with the Dusters themselves taking out some of their own people in the circular firing squad." Crescenz shook his head. "Sir, we just don't have the numbers."

Staff Sergeant William Zuiderveld stuck his head in Ames's office just then and saluted. "Excuse me, Sirs!"

"What is it, Sergeant?" Ames asked, returning the salute.

"I'm sorry to interrupt," Zuiderveld said, "but we seem to have hit on something. Duster casualties just skyrocketed."

"Show me."

Zuiderveld led Ames and Crescenz to the motion-detector room. Corporal Victoria Vifquain stood at attention.

"As you were," Ames said. "Sergeant Zuiderveld says you have something to show us, Corporal?"

"Yes, Sir!"

She pointed at the motion detectors, the NAU forces in yellow, the Dusters in red, including their ground vehicle.

The Dusters were all closer to the firebases they had surrounded, but their formation was exactly the same. In particular, the devastating ground vehicles had not changed course or direction, even though there was nothing in their path anymore.

Meanwhile, the NAU soldiers and Marines had all changed position to hit the Dusters themselves. Casualties were still awful, but they'd been lessened since the NAU had adjusted.

"Sir, I don't think anyone's driving those things," Vifquain said. "They're on a preprogrammed course, and the Dusters are staying near it for cover, but—" She shrugged. "I mean, there can't be anyone at the wheel, can there? They'd have, y'know, *turned* by now."

To Crescenz, Ames said, "Ping all personnel on the ground at all three firebases. Keep it up. Ignore the ground vehicles, and just stay out of its way. Focus on the Dusters themselves and just treat the tanks like an obstacle."

"On it!"

The airspace over Shapland

"Let's do it, Hell Raisers," Lieutenant Colonel Courtney said into the command freq for Marine Attack Squadron 121.

They only had the nine AV16C Kestrels left after their last engagement with the Dusters, but Courtney had been aching for a rematch.

Luckily, the orders came in. VMA 121 was to engage the Dusters that were surrounding the three firebases.

Courtney continued as the Kestrels took off: "Our targets are those RVs the Dusters have whipped out. Ground-based artillery isn't cutting it, so let's show those ground-pounders what we can do from the sky."

From the copilot seat in front of him, Lieutenant Power muted the freq and then said, "Uh, Sir? If Pentzer's lasers and the hand weapons can't do the trick, what makes higher-higher think our Hades guns can cut it?"

While Courtney saw where Power was coming from, and was glad he didn't say that on open comms, he also didn't appreciate the questioning. "Eyes forward, Marine."

"Aye-aye, Sir."

The truth was, they didn't have much of a chance, and they also ran the risk of losing the rest of VMA 121 after having almost half of them taken out in their last engagement.

But it made no sense for 121 to sit on their asses, either. In a war, you didn't keep your weapon holstered, and the nine remaining Kestrels were pretty damned effective weapons—too effective to be stuck in Schilt collecting dust.

Besides, Courtney wasn't the only one itching for a rematch with the Dusters. Despite cracked ribs, Captain Bruce insisted on going out, against the advice of the chief medical officer. ("It's going in your jacket that you went back on duty AMA," Dr. Frances Cunningham had said, and then she'd added, "It can go with all the other AMAs in pretty much every Marine's jacket on this planet." She'd rolled her eyes while she'd said it, too.) Captain Henry S. Huidekoper of Thirteen had gone through Boot Camp with Captain James R. O'Beirne of the destroyed Fourteen.

And while Courtney wasn't supposed to know that the pilot and copilot of Seven, Captain Emisire Shahan and First Lieutenant Wilma Hawkins, were sleeping with, respectively, the copilot and pilot of Eleven, the truth was that both Captain V.P. Twombly and First Lieutenant Alexandra S. Webb had revenge on their minds, too.

At least the planes were in tip-top shape. Staff Sergeant Fry and his grease monkeys did their jobs well, and everything was patched up and ready to go. He'd replaced a fuel line in Courtney's own Kestrel One, and all the other wounded birds were ready to fly again.

Having said that, Power was right about one thing: the Hades guns weren't going to cut it any more than anything else NAU forces had tried against the Duster vehicle.

The scatter-blast cluster-bombs, on the other hand...

They had nine Kestrels and three firebases to support, so it was easy enough to split them in threes.

"Sound off," Courtney said to make sure everyone was on the ball. "Team Beta."

Bruce's copilot, First Lieutenant Carla Ludwig, said, "Two on the way to Cart." Bruce herself had a sore throat from her wounds, so Ludwig was doing all the talking for Two.

Under other circumstances, Courtney would have told Bruce to listen to the doctor, but they couldn't spare anyone right now.

Besides, they were Marines. Cracked ribs were no different than a paper cut.

Three and Eight also reported that they were headed to Firebase Cart.

Courtney nodded, then said, "Team Gamma."

"Nine for Gasson," Captain Moses Luce said in his quiet drawl, while Captain Twombly was much more animated when he reported, "Eleven en route to Gasson." Captain Huidekoper likewise said, "Thirteen on the way to Gasson."

Fifteen and Sixteen were accompanying Courtney to Westermark. They were the only two Kestrels who didn't have at least a captain running things, as they'd taken too many casualties. Instead, both pilots were first lieutenants (with NCOs from Fry's ground crew serving as wingmen), and so they got to go along with the CO.

When Courtney said, "Team Alpha," both first looies, Bart Diggins and Louis P. Di Cesnola, acknowledged that they were following One.

Diggins simply replied, "Fifteen on the way to Westermark."

"Sixteen on Bart's tail, Sir," Di Cesnola said, and Courtney could hear the young officer's perpetual grin over comms. Nothing ever got that young man down, not even the casualties they'd suffered. Whenever someone asked why he was always in such a good mood, he always said the same thing: "I'm in the Corps, what the hell's there *not* to be happy about?"

"Give 'em hell, Hell Raisers," Courtney said. "Oo-rah!"

"*Oo-rah!*" came the response from all eight of the other planes.

Courtney flew his Kestrel toward Westermark, which was the farthest of the three from Schilt. Fifteen and Sixteen trailed behind.

"Shit," came Twombly's voice over the command freq. Gasson was closest to Schilt, so Nine, Ten, and Thirteen were already on site.

"Report, Gamma."

"Sir, we got friendlies in the blast zone."

Twombly sent his visual to Courtney's board, and the lieutenant colonel saw that the Marines on the ground were engaging the Dusters and were practically on top of the target vehicle.

"Power, get on the horn to someone at Gasson, tell them to back the hell off so we can do our jobs."

"Aye-aye, Sir," Power said, and he opened a discreet freq to Gasson.

"Holding pattern till you've got a drop, Gamma," Courtney said.

"Request permission to take out some of the Dusters while we wait?" Twombly asked.

Courtney hesitated for only a second, knowing that Twombly was particularly out for blood.

But so were they all. "Granted. Watch for friendlies."

Luce replied, "Don't you worry, Colonel, we'll just be hittin' the bad guys."

As revenge-obsessed as Twombly might have been, that's how calm under fire Luce would be. A veteran of a dozen campaigns, Luce was one of the most relaxed people Courtney had ever met, but he could navigate any flying vehicle through a fogbank blindfolded and still land right in the center of a runway.

So long as Luce's calmer head prevailed, the Gasson group would be fine.

Meanwhile, Courtney, along with Fifteen and Sixteen, did a recon run over Westermark. He saw that the Dusters' vehicle was surrounded by Dusters, but no Marines or soldiers were anywhere nearby.

Good.

Switching to local freq, Courtney said, "Alpha, ready drop, acknowledge."

"Fifteen ready," Diggins said.

Di Cesnola replied, "Rockin', rollin', and ready, Sir."

"One, two, three, on my mark," Courtney ordered.

The Kestrels flew up and around and made a second run over Westermark, flying in a straight line: One, then Fifteen, then Sixteen, about a thousand feet apart. Each would drop their load of bombs one at a time.

That last part had been suggested by Major Kawamura at Schilt. It was just a theory, but something as hard to get through as whatever the Dusters made that tank from was more likely to buckle from repeated smaller blasts rather than one big one.

Of course, "more likely" didn't mean much when they had no clue what the thing was made of or how to destroy it, but it was better than a poke in the eye with a sharp stick.

Courtney watched his HUD waiting for just the right moment to drop the cluster-bombs, and then said, "One, drop!"

Power let the bombs loose, activating the undercarriage doors that held the bombs in place.

"Break!" Courtney then said. The other part of the battle plan was to climb as high as possible as soon as the bombs dropped to give the Kestrels the best chance of not being blown out of the sky by Duster AA guns.

"Fifteen, drop!" came the voice of Diggins, and he dropped his load as well.

Diggins's copilot said, "Break!" and Fifteen started its climb.

"Sixteen, dr— Shit!" Di Cesnola cut himself off, and Courtney saw why a moment later.

Duster AA guns were firing right at him.

To Di Cesnola's credit, Sixteen dropped its load before it blew up, killed by the Dusters.

Power muttered, "Gonna miss that asshole's smile."

"Sir," Diggins said, "you seein' what I'm seein'?"

Courtney checked his HUD. It showed a huge hole in the roof of the ground vehicle.

Ludwig broadcast on the command freq. "Beta reporting success, Sir. Raised the roof, and the sucker's not moving."

"Good work, Beta."

Luce then said, "Marines on the ground have finally backed off. We remonstrated with a few aliens while we were loungin' around, though. About to begin—"

Then Luce was cut off.

Shit. "Gamma, report! Gamma! Luce, Twombly, Huidekoper, report!"

"Sir," Power said, "not picking up any of Gamma. Gasson's reporting that they've all been shot down."

Bruce's raspy voice then sounded over comms. "Sir, Beta just did a flyover of target—it's empty, Sir."

Diggins said, "Confirmed with Alpha target—no signs of *any* life in the Dusters' RV."

They'd already lost four more Kestrels, and they'd also completed their mission, so Courtney said, "Let the ground pounders worry about the cleanup. Back to base, double time!"

Firebase Cart

Corporal Joseph Frantz slowly moved toward the no-longer-moving ground vehicle, stepping over corpses of both Dusters and humans—though, he was happy to see, there were a lot more Duster bodies.

"Fuck!" came a voice from behind him, followed by the report of weapons fire.

Turning, Frantz saw PFC Du Pont had just discharged his weapon at one of the bodies.

"It twitched, Sir."

"Until it actually aims a weapon at you, save your ammo, Private. As it is, that's coming out of your allowance."

"Yes, Sir."

Normally Frantz would have been fine with Du Pont firing at an enemy who wasn't entirely dead yet. He remembered a very old movie that his mother loved, where a character referred to the difference between mostly dead and all dead—mostly dead meant partly alive and still able to be revived. The enemy needed to be all dead, otherwise, they were still targets.

But NAU forces were also depressingly low on ammunition, and if this kept up much longer before they got resupply, they were going to have to start throwing rocks at the Dusters.

Assuming they even *got* resupply. Frantz was genuinely concerned that the suits back on Earth would decide to just write off Troy as the 18th victims of the Dusters and not send any more good people to die.

What especially pissed Frantz off was that he could totally understand that theoretical point of view. If he had been one of the suits back on Earth, he might well consider the need just to cut their losses on Troy.

Let's hope I'm a bigger asshole than they are, he thought as he approached the vehicle.

The 121st had done a number on the roof, finally breaking through the seemingly impenetrable hull. His line to Du Pont before about looking a gift horse in the mouth still held, though. They had to clear the vehicle before they could declare it no longer a factor.

As soon as he reached the base of the tank, his soldiers right behind him, he confirmed that there were no hostiles still breathing around.

"Quinlan, Du Pont, Bourke, get up there."

The three privates got to work. PFC James Quinlan got a grappling hook out of his pack and attached it to a rope that Du Pont provided. He then handed it to John Gregory Bourke, who holstered his weapon and then twirled the rope and threw it up to the roof of the tank.

The hook caught on the big hole that the 121st had made with ease. Bourke tugged on it and smiled. "Easy as 3.14159."

"Say what, Greg?" Du Pont asked. Bourke hated being called "John."

"It's math humor," Quinlan said. "Easy as pi."

"That supposed to be funny?" Du Pont asked.

"Only to folks with more than one brain cell," Bourke said as he tugged one more time on the rope, then started to climb up.

"Du Pont left his brain cell on Earth," Quinlan said. "S'why he fired on that dead Duster."

"Fuck you, Jimmy," Du Pont said, but he was smiling ruefully.

Frantz knew that Du Pont wouldn't make that mistake twice, and his fellows razzing him reassured him that everyone still trusted him. After all, you didn't give shit to someone you didn't trust.

First Du Pont, then Quinlan climbed up the rope. Du Pont was halfway up when Bourke hit the roof, and he immediately unholstered his rifle and pointed it down into the gaping hole in the roof.

"Sonofa— Clear!"

Frantz looked up in surprise. He hadn't even gone down into the thing yet. "Say again, Bourke?"

"Clear—there's nothing here."

Du Pont had made it to the top and was also peering down with his weapon at the ready. "Wow, this— Corporal, you gotta see this."

Frantz had intended to wait until the privates completely cleared the vehicle before going in himself, but it seemed they already had.

Holstering his weapon and gripping the rope, he climbed up the side of the tank. The metal was unyielding under his boots, and he wondered just what the hell the Dusters made this damn thing out of.

He got to the top and peered down through the jagged hole that was pretty much all that was left of the vehicle's top.

Inside was a great deal of machinery of a design he'd never seen before.

And that was it. No bodies, no Dusters, not even any chairs or places for a living being to stand or sit or lay down or *anything*.

Just equipment.

"No wonder this thing was just firing straight ahead," Frantz muttered. "It's completely automated. Not even remote-controlled, they just pointed it at the firebase and had it shoot until it was done."

"Well, maybe it was being controlled," Du Pont said, "and the guy controlling it is one of those DBs down below."

"Maybe. Either way, let's secure this thing. The nerds at the Corps of Engineers are gonna want a gander at this sucker."

15

Combat Action Center, Battleship NAUS Durango

Radarman 2 Michael McCormick gulped down the last of his tea and stared at the screen, which continued to show him the same nothing it had all along.

But he had to keep staring. At this stage of the action in and above Troy, the job of keeping an eye on the radar was at once the most boring and the most important.

Most boring because nothing had happened since the last batch of Dusters came through.

Most important, because something *could* happen, and if and when it did, they needed to know immediately.

When *Durango* first arrived at Troy, everyone had been caught off-guard by the Duster ships that appeared from behind Troy's moon, nicknamed Mini Mouse. But that was when they didn't know what to expect from their trip to Troy—their job was, after all, to find out what, exactly, had happened.

Now, though, they had to keep a sharp eye out.

The radar station that was pointed at the location through which the Dusters' wormhole had opened each time they'd arrived was staffed by two people at all times, though McCormick was alone for the moment because Radarman 3 John F. Bickford was in the head.

Making it more boring, but no less important, was that they had a twelve-hour duty shift.

All things being equal, *Durango* functioned on three eight-hour watches, but with some personnel killed in action, others rotated to the surface to replace personnel KIA down there, shortages forced some stations into two twelve-hour watches instead.

Since the physical requirements of staffing radar were minimal, it was one of those cut from three to two.

Bickford came back in from the head, nodding to Chief Petty Officer James W. Verney and taking his seat next to McCormick.

"Everything come out okay?" McCormick asked.

Shuddering, Bickford asked, "You gotta ask that *every* time, Mike?"

"I just don't want to slip on your piss when I go."

"Don't worry. I held it nice and steady just for you."

Behind them, Verney said, "Jesus H., you guys gotta do this comedy routine *every* time one of you goes to the head?"

McCormick shrugged. "It's our way of breaking up the monotony, Chief."

"What, with more monotony? Smart plan, Radarman."

"I never said it was a *good* way." McCormick turned to grin at the chief.

Bickford added, "That's why we're lowly radarmen."

"But why are we called that?" McCormick asked.

In a very slow, deliberate tone, as if speaking to a four-year-old, Bickford said, "Because we're the men who run the radar."

"Well, first of all, I think Davidson would object to the first part," McCormick said, referring to Radarman 3 Andrea Davidson, who had McCormick's spot on the other watch.

Verney said, "'Radarwoman' and 'radarperson' have too many syllables. And Davidson, I know for a fact, doesn't give a fuck."

"Right, but that brings us to the first half of the word." As he spoke, McCormick got up and walked over to the recycler and tossed the used teabag in his mug into it.

Holding his hands palms-up, Bickford asked, "What the hell's wrong with that? You work at the radar station. What else are we supposed to be called?"

"But it's not radar, really."

Verney rolled his eyes. "Oh, here we go again."

Bickford shot a look at the chief. "Again?"

"You used to be on second watch, Bickford, and McCormick here was on first, so you've been spared his stupid rants. Until now, that is."

McCormick wanted more tea, but he wasn't about to leave the CAC for the galley until he was done with his rant. Especially now that the chief had baited him.

"How," Bickford asked, his arms now folded, "is it not radar?"

"Radar's actually an acronym for radio detection and ranging."

"That's a pretty crappy acronym," Bickford said. "Shouldn't it be RDR?"

"Talk to the U.S. Navy circa World War II. The Royal Air Force went with radio azimuth direction and ranging, but that's worse 'cause most people don't know what an azimuth is."

"Most people don't know that radar's an acronym, either," Bickford said, "so what difference does it make what it stands for?"

"Because of *what* it stands for. We haven't used radio signals for detection in ages, certainly not since we went into space. Lasers are way more efficient because light's faster than sound, and space is so big that we need the speed so the info gets to us in a timely manner."

This time Bickford rolled his eyes. "Gee, it's a good thing you told me that, Pete, 'cause I was asleep during training."

"Well, that certainly explains your aptitude rating," Verney said with a cheeky grin.

"Thanks, Chief," Bickford drawled, then turned back to McCormick. "Besides, so what? Language adjusts—it always has. When you record something visually, you still say you film it, even though nobody's used film in ages. And what we do here is the same type of thing that the old radar systems in World War II did, only better and faster—but it does the same basic thing, so it has the same name. So what's the big deal?"

McCormick just stared at Bickford for several seconds, his mouth hanging open.

The brief silence was broken by Verney's laughter. "Damn, I shoulda put you on watch with McCormick sooner. You're the first person to shut him up this whole tour."

Both radarmen chuckled, and McCormick said, "Chief, request permission to hit Radarman Bickford on the head with my tea mug."

"Denied—you might break the mug, and a new one isn't in the budget, and if you don't have your tea, you're even *more* of a pain in the ass."

Grinning, McCormick then said, "In that case, permission to get more tea."

Before the chief could reply, Bickford said, "Got a reading!"

All thoughts of tea abandoned, McCormick scrambled into his seat next to Bickford. The radar—misnamed though it may have been—had picked up readings consistent with a wormhole opening. And it was in the same relative location as the last two Duster wormholes.

Verney tapped the intercom and said, "Mess hall, CAC. Lieutenant Hudner, you're needed."

Thomas J. Hudner, the head of the radar division, ran in a few moments later. Protocol kept Verney from pointing out that the lieutenant had a bit of mustard from the lunch the chief had interrupted on his chin.

"What's happening, Chief?" Hudner asked

"Radarman McCormick, report to the lieutenant," Verney said.

"Sir," McCormick said, "we've got a Duster wormhole, and now we're picking up indications of objects coming through. Based on previous data, we should have confirmation in six minutes."

Hudner wasted no time, but activated the intercom. While doing so, he wiped off the mustard with his wrist, which relieved Verney.

"Bridge, CAC."

The first time they encountered the Dusters, the watch officer on the bridge was Lieutenant Commander Allen Buchanan, who'd sounded almost bored.

Buchanan had been reassigned to the surface to administrate the field hospital, as his previous assignment was administration at the Saxton Naval Hospital on Luna. To Hudner's surprise, the watch officer was Captain Huse his own self, who said, "CAC, bridge. What's happening, Mr. Hudner?"

Not expecting to hear directly from the captain, Hudner swallowed and said, "Wormhole opening with more Dusters coming in, Sir. We should have numbers in five minutes."

"Sound general quarters," Huse said, "Meteors, get ready to launch, and someone wake up Admiral Avery."

Admiral's Bridge, Durango

Rear Admiral James Avery once again studied the big board. There were twenty-seven blips on the right-hand side, indicating the Dusters that had come through the wormhole.

On the left was what was left of Task Force 8.

Captain Huse said, "Radar room reporting that enemy vessels are all the same size."

That got Avery to turn and face the captain of the ship. "Say again, Captain?"

"This isn't a fleet, it's a battle group. They're all small craft, moving in a single formation."

"No support vessels, no motherships?"

"That's what they're telling me." Huse pointed at the big board. "And look at those blips—they're all the same size."

The tactical display on the big board generally had larger blips for bigger craft—as an example, the blip for the *Durango* was the largest on the board—but Huse was correct in that the Duster markers were the same size. Avery had assumed that to be due to a lack of data, as the Dusters were still several light-minutes away.

But no, they really were all the same size. "Just a bunch of fighters?"

"Looks like," Huse said.

The board showed several Meteors launching from the *Norman Scott*—many fewer than the last time they engaged the Dusters.

"Laser batteries, stand by," Avery said.

Lieutenant Commander George Davis relayed those orders to the *Scott*, the only capital ship they had left.

Chief Henry Finkenbiner said, "Laser batteries standing by."

Then two of the blips disappeared.

"What the hell was that?"

Finkenbiner peered at the display at the weapons console. "Sir, we no longer have a firing solution on enemy vessels designated seventeen and twenty-four."

"Did someone fire on them?" Avery asked angrily.

"Meteors not in range," Davis said, "and neither we nor the *Scott* have fired."

Huse added, "Radar room confirms heat signatures consistent with enemy ships exploding."

Avery shook his head. "What the hell just happened?"

"Meteors thirty seconds from optimum firing range," Finkenbiner said by way of reminding Avery that he still had to give the order to fire batteries.

"Thank you, Chief. Fire batteries."

The lasers fired from both *Durango* and *Scott* and struck four of the enemy targets.

Three of them went the same way as the two that had seemingly spontaneously exploded.

"Meteors engaging," Finkenbiner said at the same time that Lieutenant Julius Townsend said, "Enemy firing."

Two more Duster blips disappeared without warning.

"Bridge, CAC," came the voice of Lieutenant Hudner over the intercom.

Huse said, "CAC, bridge, report."

"Sir," Hudner said, "we're reading several of the Duster ships venting atmo—including the two that just went boom."

"Which ones?" Avery asked.

"Ah, two, nine, eleven, twenty, and twenty-seven."

Turning to Davis, Avery said, "Tell Cromwell to have the Meteors focus their fire on every ship *but* those five. We can turn on the wounded later, but let's focus on the ones that have a better shot at taking us down."

"Aye-aye, Sir," Davis said and relayed the order to the *Scott*'s CAG.

Even as he did so, three more enemy ships exploded.

That still left twenty-one Duster vessels, and they fired back.

Avery now focused entirely on the big board as he saw the Dusters fire their laser batteries on the irritatingly few remaining Meteors.

"Batteries recharged," Finkenbiner said.

"Fire," Avery ordered.

Avery was pleased to see that, while his side suffered some losses, the enemy suffered many more, and within a few minutes, there were only seven Duster fighters left intact, and two of them were drifting.

To Davis, Avery said, "Have Cromwell tow fifteen and nineteen in." Those were the two that were drifting.

"Aye-aye," Davis said, and relayed the order.

Townsend said, "Fifteen is firing!"

Before Avery could say anything, fifteen exploded without having fired.

"Bridge, CAC." It was Hudner again. "Sirs, the heat signature was much greater on fifteen. I think the weapons malfunctioned."

"We'll take what we can get," Huse muttered.

Avery shook his head. "What the hell are they throwing at us, their surplus ships? Boats that were in the repair yard? Rejected designs?"

"All of the above?" Huse asked.

One of the Meteors was now towing nineteen. The other Meteors exchanged fire with the remaining Duster ships.

In a few more minutes, it was over. The Dusters were all killed, save the one being towed, and the NAU losses were lighter than Avery had feared.

"Comm," he said to Davis, "get General Bauer on the horn. If this is the best the Dusters can do for reinforcements, we might have a shot at winning this thing."

Farmhouse near Jordan, Eastern Shapland

LANCE CORPORAL INOUYE LED FIRST TEAM TO THEIR DESIGNATED SPOT, HAVING been given instructions by Sergeant Denig of Force Recon as to where the latter's people were, and then been given orders by Sergeant O'Donoghue as to where to set up.

Inouye's team was to enter the farmhouse first, followed by five more teams to secure the location.

They still didn't know if there were just a few Dusters in there or a whole battalion, but Inouye figured that they knew they were surrounded at this point.

Not that the Marines *actually* surrounded them. They were hardly going to make the same mistake the Dusters made around the firebases.

No, they were in a semicircle around the front entrance, with two teams in reserve around the rear in case the Dusters decided to try to sneak out the back door. Not that there *was* a back door, but they'd done enough tunneling that Lieutenant Commiskey didn't want to take any chances. They needed to be ready for anything, including a ton of Dusters firing at them all at once.

For his part, Inouye just didn't want to die.

He had lived his entire life in fear of him and his entire family dying. Service was in his blood—his mother was a sergeant in the

Honolulu Police Department, and his father was a firefighter in the same Hawai'ian city. All four grandparents served as well: Tutu Mark and Tutu Anna were both in the Army, Tutu Tommy was a Marine, and Tutu Yvonne joined the Navy.

When he was eight years old, an HPD detective came to the house and informed him and his father that his mother had been wounded in the line of duty. She'd survived that, and went back to work a few months later, though she stayed in administrative duties from that point forward. But the gut-twisting fear that his mother was dying never left young Daniel.

From that day forward, he lived in constant fear of losing everyone he loved and of dying himself, that his mother would get shot again (never mind that she was on desk duty), that his father would die in a fire, or that any of his grandparents would be killed in combat. Even though, by the time he turned eighteen, his mother was comfortably riding a desk, and his father had retired after twenty years on the job, and all four tutus were no longer on active duty, the fear didn't go away.

He felt there were only two ways to confront those fears. One was music. Inouye had a great singing voice, and he loved to use it.

The other was to become a Marine himself.

It was, on the face of it, an insane notion. But he also did some research that revealed some very simple math: the vast majority of the people who signed up for the armed forces—or to be police officers or firefighters, for that matter—did not die on the job. Indeed, the chances of doing so were about one in a million, as long as the NAU wasn't in a declared state of war.

As a private in Third Platoon, he saw no action outside of training. There was plenty of it in training, of course, but none of it was life-threatening, though it did involve being *ready* for something life-threatening.

Then he got promoted to lance corporal.

Two days later, the NAU got sucked into a war against these crazy-ass aliens.

The whole idea was working up until then, he thought dolefully.

But he didn't let the rest of the team know that. They just knew him as the guy who liked to sing a lot. In fact, he spent most of the downtime on the trip to Troy and between engagements on the planet regaling the rest of third platoon with songs. He crooned lovely renditions of many popular songs from the past few years: "One Hour Too Far," "Planetfall," "Love Will Let You Down," and "Vitamin Star."

One time, Vargas asked him to sing, "Tiny Bubbles," and in response, Inouye did an off-key version of Vargas's favorite song, "Layla," and Vargas stopped making him sing stupid Hawaiʻian songs after that. Though he did hit him with crap like the chickenshit joke...

Corporal Vincent Capodanno signaled for them to enter. Inouye went first, gun raised, entering the farmhouse's large vestibule. To the left was a dining room and kitchen, to the right a large living area, and directly in front was a staircase to the second level and a door that went to the basement.

Capodanno, Vargas, and the new guy, Okubo, all entered behind him, and they took up positions. Second team, fifth team, and eighth team followed right behind.

Eighth team then moved to secure the upstairs, as planned.

Just as the last private from eighth hit the stairs, the basement door flew open.

Inouye fired instinctively, as they'd already gotten the report from Force Recon that there were Dusters inside, possibly in the basement.

Hesitation got you someone visiting your parents' house to tell them you're dead.

The first Duster through the door went down immediately from Inouye's fire, but there were a dozen more behind that one, and they came *pouring* through the door all at once, weapons blazing.

On the one hand, it was a crazy stunt, and risky with this many Marines around.

On the other hand, even as Inouye was firing, he saw Vargas, Okubo, and Capodanno all get shot.

Then, after a few minutes, the shooting just stopped, as no more Dusters came through. Someone shouted for a corpsman as Inouye headed for the basement door.

His initial estimate of a dozen Dusters was wrong—he only counted seven Duster corpses on the floor. But the way they jinked about combined with the cramped space made it seem like there were more.

Sergeant Ruiz had entered at some point during the mêlée, along with several corpsmen to care for the wounded. Inouye noted that Okubo was still breathing, but he wasn't sure about Capodanno and Vargas.

Grieve later. At least he was still in one piece.

Ruiz spoke *sotto voce* into the discreet battalion freq. "Inouye, Bresnahan, Gurke, Kephart, check the basement. Eighth team, inform when you clear the top floor. Secure the ground floor."

Inouye wasn't sure why there was any need for Ruiz to be so quiet, given that there was plenty of noise, and stealth was pretty much out the window at this point.

Then again, shouting wasn't always heard, especially with eighth team upstairs. If it was on comms, everyone was guaranteed to hear it.

Inouye tried not to think about the fact that Bresnahan and Gurke were from second team and Kephart from fifth. Besides, they all had the same training.

Since the other three were PFCs, Inouye took point as the ranking Marine. He gingerly stepped over the Duster corpses and headed to the staircase.

He slowly padded down the stairs, weapon raised, casting his eyes back and forth. The basement was dimly lit by a far-away source.

Pointing to the night-vision visor on his helmet, he then pulled it down. He heard the other three do likewise a second later.

The entire basement became a much clearer, albeit entirely green-tinged, tableau, as the visor conveyed images via how much heat they gave off rather than how much light they reflected.

All he got for heat signatures, though were five ovoid shapes on one of the workbenches, which was along the far wall—no other signs of life.

No, wait, there was one thing—residual heat on the floor leading back—to a tunnel!

Hitting comms, Inouye said, "Hey, luna, we got no enemy contact, but we have some weird objects, and a tunnel leading north. Tunnel's been dug out of the basement wall."

Gurke muttered, "Regular buncha gophers, we got."

Ruiz's voice crackled over the speakers. "Roger that. Investigate tunnels."

Inouye pointed at Gurke and Bresnahan and then at the tunnel. Let *them* take point.

They nodded and moved forward.

PFC James Kephart said, "Uh, Danny?"

Inouye looked over at Kephart, who was inspecting the round shapes. "Yeah?"

"Um, I think these are eggs."

"Say what?"

"Eggs. And I ain't talkin' the kind you scramble, I'm talkin' the kind that turns into bouncing baby Dusters."

"Shit." He hit comms again. "Sergeant, I think we're looking at a creche here."

For a moment, there was no response, and Inouye was worried that comms were out.

"Say again, Corporal?"

"We've got what looks like five eggs down here." He looked more closely at the workbench and noticed that there were strips of cloth arranged around the shapes, like napkins next to plates on a dining room table. "It looks like a nest, Sarge. That's what they were setting up here. It's a goddamn nursery!"

Upstairs, Ruiz shook his head in amazement. *Middle of a goddamn war and they're making babies?*

He contacted Corporal Paul J. Wiedorfer of seventh team, which was one of the two out back. "Seventh team, any activity?"

Wiedorfer glanced over at PFC Pedro Cano, who held the scanner.

At first, Cano shook his head no, but then he said, "Hold up."

"Stand by," Wiedorfer said to Ruiz.

"Pickin' up movement," Cano said.

After Wiedorfer relayed that to Ruiz, the sergeant said, "We've got a tunnel in the basement leading away from the house. That's probably them. I want Seventh to follow and engage if you can."

"On it."

Once, Wiedorfer had made the mistake of saying, "Yes, Sir" to Ruiz. But only once. Ruiz made his displeasure felt in multiple ways. "Don't let these stripes fool you, Corporal, I fucking *work* for a living."

Wiedorfer had almost made the mistake of responding to *that* with "Yes, Sir," but stopped himself just in time, though he almost choked on it. Saying "Yes, Sir" to superior officers was second nature for a Marine who'd survived Boot.

But as far as Ruiz was concerned, he was a Leatherneck just like the rest of them, even with the three stripes on his sleeve.

Since both seventh team and ninth team were guarding the rear—seventh on the west side of the farmhouse, ninth on the east—Ruiz had specified that Wiedorfer's team was to go after the Dusters that were scampering underground, leaving Ninth to hold position in case something else happened behind the farmhouse.

There was nobody around aside from the Dusters Cano was picking up, but it still paid to be operationally secure, so Wiedorfer didn't raise his voice to shout across the way to where ninth team was positioned to the east of the farmhouse. Instead, he pointed at Corporal Britt Slabinski, then pointed to the ground, then pointed at himself and then at the way north.

Slabinski gave him a thumb's up in reply.

Secure in the knowledge that Slabinski would reposition his people for maximum coverage once seventh team moved out, Wiedorfer pointed at Cano, indicating he should take point, since he had the scanner.

Lance Corporal George W. Roosevelt followed close behind Cano. While the latter was good enough to switch from his scanner to his weapon in a second or two, that span could be an eternity when you were under fire yourself. So Roosevelt backed him up.

PFC Matthew S. Quay was the worst shot in the team, so he got the big shotgun and took up the rear to cover the team's six.

Cano, Wiedorfer noted, was heading straight toward a well.

Directly underneath seventh team, Inouye and his group followed down the tunnel. Inouye had no idea how the Dusters excavated this passage—there was no evidence of tool use to make these big burrows in the ground—but however they did it, the tunnel was stable and smooth as possible given that it was made of compacted dirt.

The whole notion freaked Inouye out a little bit. Growing up in Hawai'i, he was used to open spaces. Nobody on the island of O'ahu had basements, and Inouye had never even been in an enclosed space until he went to Boot. That was another reason why he had Gurke and Bresnahan take point.

However, he followed them in due course, telling Kephart, "Stay here, guard these suckers."

"Okay, but—I mean, they're just eggs."

"No, they're these people's kids, and trust me, ain't nobody in this universe crankier than a mother protecting her young. Dusters may not be the same, but they may, and it ain't worth the risk. Guard those things with both eyes open."

"Don't wink, got it," Kephart said with a cheeky grin.

Rolling his eyes, Inouye jogged to catch up with Gurke and Bresnahan.

As soon as Inouye got to them, Gurke pointed ahead. "You hear that?" he whispered.

The weird brushing sound of the Dusters' jinking movements over dirt. Inouye had heard that way too much since they landed on Troy.

"Let's double-time it."

Top-side, Wiedorfer, Cano, Quay, and Roosevelt set up around the well. Sure enough, half a dozen Duster started to scamper up the sides. They saw the four Marines and turned tail and ran back the way they came.

"Did you see any weapons on them?" Wiedorfer asked.

All three PFCs shook their heads.

"Civilians, maybe?" Roosevelt asked. "Prob'ly why they were running."

Down below, Inouye raised his weapon when he saw six Dusters coming toward them, but they stopped short and ceased movement.

"They ain't armed," Gurke said.

"I noticed," Inouye replied.

He looked beyond the Dusters to see another hole in a wall that led to a place that was getting some sunlight.

"If I remember right," Bresnahan said, "that's the well over there."

A rope dropped from above just beyond the hole, and then Roosevelt landed with a squish. Inouye noted that the lance corporal was up to his ankles in water, which made sense if that was a well.

The Dusters continued not to move.

Roosevelt said, "They turned tail and ran just lookin' at us up top. Now they ain't movin'."

Inouye nodded. "Yeah." He activated comms and said, "Sergeant Ruiz, seventh team and the tunnel crew just captured us six unarmed Dusters. We, um, we think they're surrendering."

"Corporal, please confirm, unarmed Dusters surrendering?"

"Confirming unarmed—surrendering is a guess. I mean, they're not raising their arms or waving a white flag or anything, but they're aliens. They're just, y'know, *standing* there."

"All right, Corporal, secure them and bring them back to the farmhouse."

"Will do." Inouye also knew better than to "Sir" the sergeant. "Let's bundle us up some prisoners."

Inside the Command Bunker, Firebase Gasson

CAPTAIN PATRICIA PENTZER WATCHED HER STATUS BOARD IN HORROR AS SHE SAW that the Duster ground vehicle was heading straight for her front door, along with a large number of Dusters.

Opening her comms to a wide freq, she cried out, "Mayday, mayday, command bunker under attack!"

Even as she did so, she whipped out her sidearm.

Behind her, Sergeant Norton did likewise. "Been a while since I fired a gun this small."

Pentzer snorted.

There was no response to her mayday, which meant that no one was available to help her. They were too busy keeping their own asses intact to have time to come save Pentzer's.

To First Lieutenants Haring and Newman, she said, "Norton and I will cover you. Keep firing at the Dusters on the other firebases."

"Yes, Ma'am," they both said in unison.

Pentzer and Norton set up in position near the front door to the bunker, which was dented and scorched from being fired upon by the Dusters.

"Think it'll hold, Cap?" Norton asked, indicating the door with his head.

"Hell if I know," Pentzer answered. "Only thing that's even slowed the Dusters' little APC, or whatever it is, down is cluster bombs. Lasers and everything else is like spitting on it. This door's good, but it's taken a pounding already, and I'm not sure it's gonna be able to keep that damn thing back."

Haring called out, "Captain?"

"Go, Haring."

"I've got good news and bad news. Which do you want first?"

Again, Pentzer snorted. "Can't remember the last time I got good news, so hit me with that."

"The Dusters attacking Cart and Westermark are in full retreat."

Despite herself, Pentzer was impressed. Even factoring in their stupid surround-the-fire-base strategy, the Dusters had numbers and willingness not to let friendly fire get in the way of victory on their side.

However, she had a feeling she could guess the bad news.

Sure enough, Haring went on: "The bad news, though, is that they're retreating here."

"Of course, they are."

Her mayday had continued to go unanswered, and the firebase was now surrounded, the Kestrels that tried to blow up the tank were killed, and now they were about to be overrun.

"I don't fancy the idea of the Dusters getting their hands on all our big guns," she said.

"Me either," Norton said.

"They got enough of an advantage."

As Pentzer spoke, she could hear the fire on the bunker intensifying. It was only a matter of time.

"They do," Norton said.

"Can anyone get Colonel Ames or Lieutenant Grieg or *someone* on comms?"

Staff Sergeant Cleto Rodriguez had taken over at communications. "I can't raise anyone on Gasson, Cap'n. All I can get from Cart and Westermark is that they're still securing their positions."

Pentzer nodded, even as the Dusters continued to pound on the bunker's walls and door.

It would be at least a few minutes before any reinforcements would get the order to come to Gasson, and it would take many more minutes for them to arrive, if not longer.

Gasson didn't have that kind of time.

"Fuck it. Engage Plan Omega."

Norton nodded. "That's the right call, Cap."

Haring and Newman both again said, "Yes, Ma'am" in unison, and they, along with their crews, started the process by which the big guns would overload and explode.

To Rodriguez, she said, "Send our intentions to General Bauer at HQ."

Swallowing loudly, Rodriguez said, "Yes, Ma'am."

About seven seconds before the Dusters busted down the bunker door, the guns exploded in a fiery conflagration. The firebase had become a literal base on fire, with flames vaporizing everyone inside as well as everyone who was right outside—which was a large number of the Dusters.

Headquarters, North American Union Forces,
near Millerton, Shapland

Lieutenant General Bauer was starting to allow himself to think that they might pull this off.

Even though it would clearly be at a most terrible cost.

He'd been collecting reports for the last hour that were guardedly encouraging.

The first was from Admiral Avery in space.

"General, we had twenty-seven Duster ships come in as reinforcements, but they didn't really reinforce all that well. Just a collection of fighters, no support, no capital ships."

That surprised Bauer. "That's it?" When he'd gotten the word that another Duster wormhole had opened, he had assumed another fleet was going to come through. This was barely even a group, much less a fleet.

"That's it. We were able to take them out with minimal losses, thank Christ. And, Harold? I swear to God, half those ships blew up all on their own."

"What's your take, Jim?"

"It is my considered opinion that the Dusters have spent the first two major engagements throwing their best at us, and they're now scraping the bottom of the barrel."

Bauer nodded. That was his take, as well. "What's your status?"

"We've got one Duster ship in tow that's depowered."

"I'll contact Captain Otani and tell his nerd squad to expect another toy to play with," Bauer said. Kazuo Otani was the commanding officer of the team from the Army Corps of Engineers assigned to Troy.

"Another?"

"We've captured two of the Dusters' tanks."

"Excellent. I'll have Captain Huse coordinate delivery of the Duster ship."

Bauer's next reports were from Colonel Ames at the firebases.

"Cart and Westermark are secure," Ames said. "Not without significant losses, but we've got two of those vehicles for Captain Otani's nerds to play with."

"A pity about Gasson," Bauer said quietly.

Ames nodded. "We couldn't secure it. Forces there were overrun, and the enemy was two steps away from capturing the base *and* its weaponry. Captain Pentzer had no choice but to Plan Omega the base."

"It was absolutely the right call, but I suspect we're gonna miss those lasers before this is over."

"Better to have them slagged than in the Dusters' hands, Sir."

"Damn right. Good work, Colonel."

Bauer's final report was from Colonel Frances Cunningham, M.D., the chief medical officer.

"Colonel, what's the casualty report?"

"Appalling," she said, wiping sweat off her brow. "We lost fifty percent of our people assigned to the firebases before Pat Pentzer decided to channel the kamikazes. We're still crawling through the wreckage there for final numbers."

The general was about to say something, but the doctor held up her hand.

"I know, General, I know, get the wounded back on duty as fast as possible."

"I'm sure you will, Colonel. What's the supply situation like?"

"Also appalling. We're low on bandages, staples, salves, painkillers, antibiotics... Honestly, it'd be faster to tell you what we're *not* low on."

Bauer took the bait. "Fine, what are we *not* low on?"

"Casualties. Think you can do something about that?"

With a sigh, Bauer shook his head. "It's war, Frances, you know—"

"Oh, for the love of Christ, don't give me the 'in war, people die' speech. I get that, but what I'm worried about right now aren't the people dying in combat, it's the ones that'll die of an infection or from some post-op complication because I don't have the right meds to give them."

"I'll see what I can get from the Navy," Bauer said.

"Yeah, I tried that, but Pym's a hoarding little shit," Cunningham said, referring to Lieutenant Commander James Pym, her equivalent with the Navy. "I used all my charm on him, and he won't give me bupkus."

"I'll give it a shot anyhow." Bauer smirked. "My charm has three stars to back it up, not just a little bird."

Cunningham smiled for the first time in a long time. "Thank you, Harry."

"Keep up the good work, Frances."

After the CMO signed off, Bauer put in a call back to *Durango*. He needed to pry more supplies out of Pym, and then figure out what crazy-ass thing the Dusters were going to try next...

Corps of Engineers Bunker,
Headquarters, North American Union Forces,
near Millerton, Shapland

MOST OF WHAT THE NAU ARMY SENT TO TROY INCLUDED SOLDIERS UNDER THE command of Major General Conrad Noll, clerical and support staff, under the command of Lieutenant Colonel Ernest von Vegesack, and medical personnel under the command of Colonel Frances Cunningham.

But there were also a hundred or so people under the auspices of the Army Corps of Engineers, commanded by Captain Kazuo Otani.

The main job of the "Aces," as they'd been nicknamed, was to build things. Upon making planetfall, the Aces—the vast majority of whom were construction workers who put up buildings and bunkers, built bridges and byways, and generally made something out of nothing under the watchful eye of Chief Petty Officer Samantha Fuqua—built everything that the NAU forces needed to run their campaign on Troy.

The main reason why it took so long for the Dusters to get through the command bunker of Firebase Gasson—thus giving Captain Pentzer time to enact Plan Omega—was because the Aces built their bunkers to *last*. Even the Dusters' devastating weaponry couldn't get completely through on one shot.

However, in addition to Fuqua's crack construction squad, the Aces also included a team of specialists under the command of

Otani's second-in-command, Lieutenant Nicky Daniel Bacon, who had acquired the nickname "Pork" at some point in his career and had yet to shake it. Where Fuqua's scaffold monkeys were all privates, Pork's team of scientists, engineers, and programmers all had the rank of specialist and were experts in their particular field.

They hadn't had much to do since making planetfall, aside from helping the Aces out in their construction work—nobody sat idle for long if they wanted to stay in the Army—and examining what little equipment they'd managed to take off the Dusters. Bacon had been genuinely concerned that they were going to go stir crazy without a proper project to occupy their time, and that usually led to a practical joke war among the group of them, which would later extend to the rest of the Aces.

Now, though, they had the mother lode, for which Bacon was grateful, as he really wasn't looking forward to waking up with an APC taken apart and reassembled in his bunk, which was what happened the last time his specialists were not given sufficiently diverting tasks to perform.

The Dusters' latest batch of reinforcements had also included their fancy new ground vehicles, and the two captured at Firebases Cart and Westermark had been brought to "the Pork Barrel," a shack that was the last item constructed by Fuqua's team on Troy as it had the lowest priority. But it was filled with all the equipment they needed to play with their toys, once they got their hands on some.

And this one was a doozy, one that would keep all thoughts of practical jokes far from the specialists' hearts and minds.

The morning after the battle at the firebases, Otani himself came out to the Pork Barrel to get a report.

Lieutenant Bacon nodded to his CO upon his entrance through the thick metal door. "Morning, Sir."

"It is that," Otani said wearily. "I'm really looking forward to this war being over so I can get a *good* night's sleep."

"Wouldn't know about that, Sir," Bacon said. "We've been up all night."

Otani blinked in surprise. "They haven't had any sack time?"

"Couldn't talk them into it, Sir. You know how they get when they've got a new toy to play with."

"And you haven't, either?"

Bacon shook his head. "When my boys and girls are left unsupervised, they get into mischief."

That prompted a snort from Otani, who also recalled the APC incident.

"So, what do we have?"

"Quite a bit, actually. Romulus and Remus have told us a great deal."

Otani let out a sigh. Having been in charge of the Aces in general and Bacon's nerds in particular for so long, he knew that the Duster vehicles wouldn't escape the custody of the Aces without being nicknamed. And given some of the loopy names they'd come up with over the years, Otani had to admit to being relieved it was something as relatively straightforward as the mythological twins who were said to have founded the Roman Empire. He still remembered the embarrassment when Specialist Josephine Cicchetti had named a vehicle they were refurbishing after a famous male stripper she was fond of, which didn't sit well with the four-star general they were refurbishing it for when his aide informed him of the nickname's provenance.

Bacon led Otani through the corridors of the Pork Barrel to the large room in the back, which had been dubbed the garage. The wide-open space barely had room to fit the two Duster vehicles.

Otani couldn't help but think that right now, they looked like packages that had been ripped open. The tops were exposed, charred, and damaged from the bombings, but the sides, front, and back remained unscathed.

He also noticed that the one on the left had "ROM" painted on the side, while the one on the right said, "REM." One pair of legs stuck out from under Romulus, another from under Remus, and Otani could hear voices from inside one of them, possibly both.

Were this a standard Army unit, Bacon would have barked, "Ten-*hut!*" and then the various specialists would fall in and stand at attention.

But these were engineers and mechanics and programmers, and expecting standard discipline from them was just asking for trouble. So Bacon just said, "Kids, Daddy's home."

Specialist Willa Alchesay, the team's mechanical engineer, turned out to belong to the legs under Remus. She slid out from under the vehicle on a rolling flat cart, wiping a smudge of dirt off her small nose. "Morning, Captain Otani!"

"Good morning, Specialist."

The legs under Romulus belonged to the structural engineer, Specialist Demetri Corahogi, which Otani only knew because he recognized the voice that cried, "Ow," followed by a stream of Russian profanity.

As she clambered to her feet, Alchesay said, "Jesus W. Christ, Dema, when you gonna learn to stop dropping the wrenches on your head?"

The remaining three members of the team were inside Remus. Each popped up from the hole in the top in sequence. Otani assumed they were using a ladder or some such that he couldn't see. A metal staircase on wheels sat against the vehicle near the engineers.

First came Cicchetti, the team's electrical engineer, her dark hair flying out in all directions despite an attempt to hold it in place with a hair tie. She'd had short hair when they'd shipped out to Troy, but it had grown to neck length just in the time they'd been there. Unfortunately, the only ones who brought a barber to Troy were the Navy, and he was in space right now.

She started to climb down the stairs, followed by the scowling face of Specialist Rodney Yano, the tactical systems expert, and the smiling face of the head programmer, Specialist Joe Rodriguez Baldonado.

"Stumble in, please," Bacon said with a smirk, and Otani chuckled.

Back when he'd first taken command of the Aces, Bacon had warned him that they weren't exactly Regular Army, and in particular, right before Otani's first inspection, had urged him not to expect them to fall in regulation-style.

Sure enough, when they had assembled for inspection, they had sort of wandered into something vaguely resembling a straight line, and not even at attention—indeed, Cicchetti and Yano had been murmuring about a laser tracking system they had been in the midst of upgrading.

"You're right, Lieutenant," Otani had said then. "They don't fall in, they stumble in."

Everyone had laughed at that, and Bacon had breathed a sigh of relief. The worst thing the Army could have done was put a hardline baton-up-the-ass military stickler in charge of a team of engineers.

But Otani understood that these were original thinkers, people who needed a chance to cut loose and do what they did best so that the people using the equipment they worked on could do their best.

"So tell me," Otani said now, "what we have here."

While they were all the same rank, Alchesay had been with the Aces longest, so she tended to be the unofficial spokesperson for the team. "As far as we can tell, Sir, it's a souped-up APC."

Otani frowned. "There were no Dusters inside the vehicles when they were captured, isn't that correct?"

"Yes, Sir," Alchesay said, confused.

"Then how, Specialist, do you all come to the conclusion that this was an armored personnel carrier when it wasn't carrying any personnel?"

"It wasn't, but it could have," she said. Reaching into the pocket of her fatigues, she pulled out a minicomputer and called up something on its display, then showed it to the captain.

Otani saw the floor of the interior of one of the vehicles, which had indentations.

"What am I looking at, Specialist?"

"Seats, Sir. I believe, and Dema—er, Specialist Corahogi concurs, that these are seats for the Dusters."

Corahogi spoke up, out of turn, of course, but that, too, was par for the Ace course. "A human would not fit properly in such a place, but I believe the Dusters would easily be able to sit and spread out comfortably while being carried."

Yano added, "It's my guess that they weren't carrying personnel, as you say, Sir, because there was no need for that part of its function. We usually use APCs to get from one place to another, but that's for engagements that are all on the same planet—hell, on the same continent. But the Dusters came from space. They got here via spaceships."

"We're thinking," Alchesay said, "that they only brought them along now instead of in the earlier engagements because they're designed for terrestrial work. But they got enough of an ass-whooping from our soldiers that they had the need to bring in the big guns."

Bacon hid a smile. That was one way in which the Aces were just like everyone else in the Army. If the NAU forces won an engagement, it was *obviously* because of the hard work of the soldiers, and the Marines and sailors just helped out a little. It was all nonsense, of course, but try telling that to any soldier—or, for that matter, any Marine who felt the same disdain toward the Army and Navy or any sailor who felt that way about the Marines and Army. Bacon figured it kept everyone sharp, knowing that they had to maintain the standard of being better than the other two services.

"And a mighty big gun it is," Alchesay added with a look at Yano.

Taking the cue, the tactical systems specialist stepped forward a bit. "Romulus here uses a beam of coherent light that fires at ten thousand megawatts."

Otani's eyes widened. The laser batteries at the firebases were at one thousand, and the most powerful laser batteries in the Navy's arsenal were only at two thousand. "No wonder this was cutting down everything in its path."

"Yes, Sir." Yano pointed at Remus. "Remus has what looks like an older model."

"You think," Alchesay put in.

"Yes, Willa, I *think*, and since this is my area of expertise—"

"The gun on Remus is smaller, more compactly designed, and has less physical wear-and-tear on it."

"Probably because they haven't used it much," Yano said. "And anyhow, the main reason why I think it's older is that it only fires at nine thousand megawatts. The newer ones are usually the more powerful ones."

"Not always—sometimes, you sacrifice power for versatility and ease of use. Everything's more streamlined on Remus's gun, and besides—it's not that much of a difference."

"Willa's got a point," Baldonado said with his trademark grin. "I mean, if you're in a building on fire, it don't matter if it's eight hundred degrees or nine hundred degrees. You're dead either way."

"Right," Alchesay said, "in terms of raw damage, it's pretty much the same, and I think they cut down a thousand megawatts so they could use the smaller aperture, which gives them—"

Otani had been willing to let them go up to a point, but it was time to yank on the reins and haul them in. "The point *is*," and then they all quieted down, "that these weapons are devastating. My next question is more important: why weren't there any personnel in it?"

The specialists all exchanged confused glances.

Bacon came to their rescue. "The captain isn't referring to the empty divots in the floor, he's referring to the lack of any kind of driver for the vehicle."

"Nowhere to sit," Alchesay said. "We haven't been able to find any kind of manual steering controls—and that's accounting for the fact that the Dusters' ergonomics would be different from ours. But all the systems we've found look like they're designed to be preset."

Baldonado jumped in again. "I was able to break into their programming—even aliens are stuck with ones and zeros when it comes to computers—and it looks to me like it's all meant to be set up and then run. Kinda like a game. Lots of if-thens, where it's designed to respond to a particular way if something happens."

"That's why we think these are meant for terrestrial engagements," Alchesay added. "It's a lot easier to preprogram something that's on your homeworld in familiar territory."

Otani nodded. "Okay, here's the big question: can you operate it?"

Baldonado said, "Absolutely" at the exact same time that Yano said, "Not a chance in hell."

There was an awkward pause, and then Otani slowly said, "At least one of you two has to be wrong."

"He is," Baldonado said.

"It would take years to figure out how to reprogram the stupid thing." Yano's voice was climbing.

Baldonado kept his tone even. "We don't *have* to reprogram it." He glanced at Otani. "I'm assuming the captain wants to know if we can turn this into a weapon for our side?"

"Affirmative."

"Then all we really need to do is set it up to go in a direction and keep shooting until it gets there."

"And how do we make it do that?" Yano asked.

"We don't have to *make* it do that. It's already *programmed* to do that. That's what the Dusters did with it at the firebases. All we have to do is figure out how to hit 'go' on it, and we're golden."

"*Chyort,*" Corahogi muttered. "He's right."

Otani turned to Baldonado. "Specialist, how long do you need to find the Duster equivalent of that 'go' button?"

"Couple hours? Maybe less if Rodney actually, y'know, *helps* instead of bitching and moaning."

Now turning to Yano, Otani said, "Specialist Yano your bitching-and-moaning privileges have hereby been revoked. Assist Specialist Baldonado in any way necessary to make these things operational."

Something occurred to Bacon as Otani was speaking. "Excuse me, Sir, but I have one other concern—what's this thing's power source?"

"We were saving that for last, Sir." Alchesay looked over at Cicchetti. "Floor's yours, Jo."

Cicchetti ran her hand through her tangled mop of hair. "I've been examining Remus's power structure, and I've found what looks like a battery. Here's the thing—it's covered in tiny little holes that, after futzing with them half the night, I've realized are absorption ports."

"What do they absorb?" Otani asked.

With a huge grin bisecting her face, Cicchetti said, "Everything. Sir, as far as I can tell. This sucker takes in anything in the vicinity and converts it to energy. Air, dust, dirt, spit, you name it—if it comes in any kind of contact with it, it gets sucked in and transformed into energy to keep it going. It's like some Duster genius figured out how to universalize a solar or wind converter. Sir, we take this back to Earth, we won't have any kind of energy problem ever again."

"And the good news there," Alchesay added, "is that we don't have to worry about Romulus or Remus losing power."

"Sir," Cicchetti said, "we've only had this thing for one night, and we've already found the most powerful semi-portable weapon in creation and a self-perpetuating battery. I get that this'll be a useful weapon to use against the Dusters, but I think I speak for all of us when I say that at least one of these guys should stay with us so we can learn more from it."

"Romulus has more powerful weaponry," Corahogi said. "Best to use it against Dusters, let us continue to learn from Remus—not just for science," he added quickly, "but to learn more about the enemy."

"Forewarned is forearmed, and all that," Alchesay put in.

"I'm fine with my two arms, thanks," Otani drawled, "but I see your point. That decision gets made over all our heads, but I'll recommend it very strongly higher-higher."

"Thank you, Sir."

"Meantime, priority is to put these monsters to *our* good use. So your assignment is to continue to be the wolves suckling Romulus and Remus so they can go found Rome."

All the Aces present chuckled, and Alchesay said, "You got it, Captain."

"Commencing howl-at-the-moon maneuver," Baldonado said, his grin widening.

Corahogi actually howled at that, and everyone laughed more.

"All right, enough," Otani said. "Get to work."

For a moment, he considered ordering them all to nap. They *had* been up all night, and they were obviously even punchier than usual.

But he also saw the glint in all their eyes. Even the usually downbeat Yano was obviously excited to get back to crawling around inside Romulus and Remus.

And they had gained incredibly valuable intel, both for the war effort and for Earth in general.

Having said that, sleep deprivation was a torture method for a reason. "Lieutenant Bacon, I want you to set up a rotation of naps for your team—make sure they at least get to reboot their brains a bit."

"Will do, Sir," Bacon said gratefully. Had he himself given the order, there was a better than even chance that the nerds would try to work around it, but coming from the captain, it would carry more weight.

For his part, Otani left the Pork Barrel trying to figure out how to convince the various majors, colonels, and generals above him to let the Aces keep one of their shiny new weapons to study longer and only give one of them back to the Army to use against their builders.

19

The Prairie Palace, Omaha,
Douglas County, Federal Zone, NAU

FLORENCE GROBERG ONCE AGAIN FOUND HERSELF SITTING IN ADMIRAL Welborn's office.

She had expected to return to the Prairie Palace as soon as her interview with the president was scheduled. However, she was not brought to the Round Office when she arrived, as expected. Nor was she taken to the Purple Room—on those rare occasions when Mills had granted a one-on-one interview, he often had it in that violet-colored space.

Instead, she was back in Welborn's place of work, staring at his pictorial history of warships. At present, she was regarding SV-41869, the prosaic designation given to the experimental military vessel that was the first to be used in space successfully, and which wound up defending Earth during the Lunar Uprising.

Public response to the Troy tragedy was mixed. President Mills had explained that the distances involved made it difficult to have proper information in a timely manner, and they didn't want to announce the invasion and its response publicly until they knew for sure that there *was* an invasion.

That, Groberg knew, was only half true, but humans had been in space long enough—and dealt with the time lag inherent in such distances—that most people bought it.

There was also significant outrage, of course, and tremendous support for the troops being sent in to avenge Troy's loss.

Welborn finally entered his office from a back door. "Sorry to keep you waiting, Ms. Groberg. The president is still willing to give you those ten minutes, but we wanted to make you a better offer."

Groberg steamed. "Are you kidding me? Admiral, I made it quite clear in this very room that the interview with the president was non—"

"How'd you like to go to Troy?"

That brought Groberg up short. "Excuse me?"

"There's a long history of embedding reporters with military units. We've been assembling reinforcements for Troy, and they're shipping out first thing in the a.m. There's a berth for you on one of the transports, if you're up for it. Since you have combat experience, you're the only reporter we really trust not to get yourself killed over there."

Opening her mouth and then shutting it, Groberg then shook her head. That was *not* what she was expecting.

It was also a great opportunity. And a terribly risky one. As a former SEAL boat captain, she knew damn well how bad things got in open combat, and these so-called "Dusters" seemed like a nastier foe than anyone SEAL Team 9 faced back in the day.

But journalistic careers were made covering combat close in like this.

"I'd have full access?"

"Well, we can do it one of two ways. Everything you write has to be subject to approval by Secretary Hobson's office. If you agree to that, you'll have full access. If you don't agree to that, you'll only be interacting with NCOs and privates and ensigns."

"Um." Groberg chuckled. "The admiral may have forgotten this from being flag rank for so long, but all the really *good* stories come from the NCOs and privates and ensigns."

"Yes, but that's *all* you'll get if you don't agree to War Department approval."

Groberg was tempted to tell Welborn to take his War Department approval and shove it where the sun didn't shine, and if she was one of a pool of reporters being embedded, she'd have done so.

But she was going to be the only journalist on Troy, at least initially, and she had a responsibility to paint the *entire* picture for the people back here on Earth who were now desperate for information about how their colony was being avenged and defended.

Which meant she needed to be able to talk to *everybody*, from the generals and admirals who were making the plans to the colonels and captains who were giving the orders to the grunts who were doing the actual work.

She was correct in that the best stories would come from the latter group, but Welborn was right that it would limit her focus too much.

Besides, she was friends with Charles Abrell, the head of public information for the War Department. He wouldn't go crazy with the redactions, just limiting it to strictly classified material. And Groberg generally knew what subjects to avoid in that regard in any case.

"All right, Admiral." She rose to her feet and offered her hand. "I'm in—full access, and full approval by Secretary Hobson's office."

Welborn returned the handshake. "Excellent."

"But I still want my ten minutes with the president. I came all this way, and I don't have to leave for Troy until morning, you said."

At that, Welborn smiled. "That's fine, Ms. Groberg. In fact, it's more than fine, it's perfect, as it means I'm now ten bucks richer."

Groberg frowned. "Excuse me?"

"Secretary Hobson thought you'd take the embedding assignment in lieu of interviewing the president. I was fairly certain you'd stick to your guns on those ten minutes."

"Can't have been *that* certain, if you only bet ten bucks." Groberg chuckled. "The Purple Room?"

"Actually, the president has a lot of work today, so he can only give you his ten minutes in the Round Office. Let's go."

Headquarters, North American Union Forces,
near Millerton, Shapland

Major General Hugh Purvis stared at Lieutenant General Harold Bauer from the screen in the latter's office.

"What's your sitrep, Hugh?" Bauer asked.

"Holding firm, but I don't know how much longer that'll be the case. Some of the Dusters are engaged with our forces in Jordan, and we're holding our own, but a lot of the survivors from the firebase conflicts have retreated into the woods of Shapland, and I think they're regrouping and getting ready to hit us again."

"Orbital recon tells us they're just sitting there," Bauer said.

Purvis nodded. "The problem is, we don't have the manpower to go in after them. They picked a thick part of the woods. Prior to the engagements at the firebases, we'd have been all over it, but our losses were too great."

"Can you reinforce with personnel from Jordan?"

Shaking his head, Purvis said, "I don't believe it will be enough to make a difference, and we'll probably lose Jordan on top of that."

"Reinforcements from Earth are due in three days."

"I'm not sure we have that, Harold." Purvis sighed. "And if they come out guns a-blazing, we might be able to hold our own, we might even win, but I don't know how many'll be left to celebrate."

"The Aces say they can have one of the Dusters' vehicles ready for our use by tomorrow. Will that help?"

"It might." Purvis sounded tentative.

Reading that as his subordinate having another idea, but not wanting to speak out of turn, Bauer cleared his throat. "What's your recommendation, General Purvis?"

Taking the cue to be more formal, Purvis said, "Sir, I recommend we divert Navy resources for orbital bombardment. The last report from Admiral Avery is that the only forces the Dusters have left to send against us are clapped-out ships that can't even hold together. The likelihood of more Dusters coming through the wormhole is minimal at this point. Task Force 8 is holding the line against an enemy that isn't coming, in my opinion. And if TF 8 can drop some Rods from God on the Dusters' location, it'll take out a big chunk of their forces in one shot. Then we can divert everyone to Jordan, including the Duster tank we've commandeered."

Bauer rubbed his chin. "I'll talk to Admiral Avery and get back to you."

"Thank you, Sir. Meantime, Force Recon is going in to try to get a better idea of what the Dusters are doing in there."

"Good. Keep up the good work, Hugh."

"Thanks, Harold."

Purvis's face disappeared from the screen, and Bauer called his aide in.

Captain William Upshur entered the office. "Sir?"

"Get me Admiral Avery."

"Yes, Sir. Dr. Cunningham's waiting outside for you."

Referring to the chief medical officer by her title instead of her rank indicated that she specifically had something medical to discuss with him. "Bring her in."

Upshur nodded and went back to his office.

Moments later, he escorted the CMO into the general's office.

"What've you got for me, Frances?"

Cunningham was wearing a white lab coat over her fatigues, and her hands were in that coat's pockets. "You know those eggs they brought back from the farm?"

Bauer nodded.

"I think—I think they're hatching."

"That is what eggs generally do," Bauer drawled.

"Thanks for that, 'cause I wasn't paying attention when we did biology in med school."

"Your sarcasm is noted, Doctor," Bauer said a bit more tightly, "but I'm not clear why you felt the need to come all the way over here to tell me that eggs are hatching."

"For starters, the Aces never bothered to build me a maternity ward. Or a NICU."

Bauer sighed. "I was under the impression that you studied xenobiology, or is that another class you didn't pay attention during?"

"Your sarcasm is noted right back," Cunningham said. "But the entire field of xenobiology is primarily theoretical at this point. And given the Dusters' similarity to certain insectoid and avian creatures, a vet would probably be better qualified than I am."

"Do the best you can, Colonel. That's all any of us are doing."

Cunningham blew out a breath. "Fine. I've got the eggs in the quarantine unit, and they'll stay there even after they hatch. No goddamn clue what to feed the little monsters, but we'll figure something out."

"If you do," Bauer said, "let Army CID know. They've taken charge of the prisoners, and we don't know what to feed them, either."

Upshur stuck his head in the office. "Excuse me, General, Colonel, but I have Admiral Avery."

Bauer regarded the CMO. "Is there anything else, Colonel Cunningham?"

"I suppose not." The doctor sighed. "I was hoping you had a better idea of how to deal with these things."

"My job isn't to take care of them, Frances," Bauer said gently, "it's to stop them."

"Yeah. All right, I'll let you know when we have some bouncing baby whatevers in quarantine."

She left with Upshur, and Bauer then activated his comm to start the conversation with Avery, whose face appeared on his screen from his office on *Durango*.

Quickly and concisely, Bauer passed on Purvis's proposal.

"I'm assuming," Avery said after Bauer finished, "that you approve of this plan as well?"

"I think it's our best chance of putting a major dent in the Dusters' forces. We've mostly had the upper hand, but only by the skin of our teeth, and only after significant losses. I'd rather deal them a vicious blow before they have a chance to catch their breath. They may be able to take us down before our reinforcements get here." Bauer hesitated. "But I need your opinion, not as your CO, but as a fellow commander. Will this leave your ass hanging the breeze?"

"Oh, I can talk to you as my CO either way, General, because your call came to me about half an hour before I was going to call you with a proposal that is eerily similar to the one General Purvis gave you." Avery gave a half-smile. "It is my opinion, based on my own experiences—and, I might add, backed up by my intelligence personnel up here—that the fleet we engaged was the last-ditch attempt by an enemy who knows that the end is near and is making one last Hail Mary pass before they lose the game."

"So, you agree that it's unlikely that you will be needed to face more Dusters coming through the wormhole?"

"I do."

"Very well, Admiral. Glad to see we're all on the same page. Send me your battle plan when it's complete, and we'll bomb the shit out of those Dusters in the woods."

"Expect the report in twenty minutes."

Once Avery signed off, Bauer had Upshur get in touch with the Aces. "Tell Captain Otani," he said, "that the Duster combat vehicles are to be assigned to Colonel Chambers at Camp Howard."

"Yes, Sir, but, um—" Upshur hesitated.

"What is it, Bill?"

Blowing out a breath, Upshur said, "Sir, the Aces want to hang on to one of the vehicles for further study. They said the tactical benefits would be massive if the nerd squad can crawl through its insides some more."

Bauer suspected that the nerd squad in question just wanted to learn more, but he also had faith in Colonel Chambers's Marines only to need the assistance of one really big gun.

"Very well, but tell the captain that the second vehicle is on standby in case things in Jordan go pear-shaped."

"Understood."

Admiral's Bridge, Battleship NAUS Durango

THE NOTION OF ORBITAL BOMBARDMENT WITH SIMPLE PROJECTILES DATED BACK to the twentieth century. The theory was that, from a high enough orbit, you simply let go of an object and let it fall. As it plummeted planetward, the kinetic energy built up so that by the time it hit its target, it impacted with the force of a bomb.

The best part was that you didn't need any kind of special equipment. You could use rocks, and it would work just as well. No need to manufacture explosives or dangerous materials.

The most efficient projectile was quickly determined back in the day to be a twenty-foot metal rod that was about a foot in diameter. The length provided a wide surface area to absorb the kinetic energy that would then be discharged on impact. The small diameter minimized friction and maximized speed.

NAU Navy capital ships were all equipped with a complement of so-called "Rods from God" that could be used for bombardment. (Several military and civilian ship designers had tried to find a way to equip smaller fighter craft with them. Unfortunately, while most bombs could be dropped from a horizontal position, the Rods from God really needed to be fired vertically to be at their most effective. The only way to equip fighters properly would be either to give them a twenty-foot rod mounted vertically on the side of the craft, which was spectacularly awkward and complicated maneuvering, or to have the pilots only be able to fire the weapon while diving toward or climbing away from the target, neither of which was optimal.)

Avery watched the big board as *Durango* moved into geo-sync orbit over the forest where the Dusters were hunkered down.

"Verify position of Marines," Avery said.

Captain Huse immediately opened a channel. "Bridge, CAC, verify position of Marines."

A moment later, Chief Verney's voice came over comms. "Marines in position three miles from forest perimeter."

"The Dusters aren't at the perimeter, Chief."

"Radar can't penetrate the forest, Sir, perimeter's the best we can do."

Avery snarled. "Davis, call the Marines—they must've sent Force Recon in to get the Dusters' position. Find it."

"Aye-aye, Sir."

Minutes later, Davis reported back with specific coordinates.

Huse sighed. "Send that to CAC. Chief Verney, based on coordinates Lieutenant Commander Davis is sending you, position of Marines relative to the Dusters, please?"

"Stand by, bridge." Verney muttered something Avery couldn't make out, then: "Estimate Marines at four-point-seven miles from Duster position."

"Chief Finkenbiner," Avery said, "give us a firing solution for the Rod from God that will give us a blast radius of three miles or less, and send it to navigation."

"Aye-aye, Sir." Finkenbiner turned to consult with the weapons techs.

While waiting for the weapons techs to do the math on what orbital position *Durango* would need to take up to drop a rod that would provide a blast radius big enough to wipe out the Dusters in the forest but small enough so it wouldn't take the Marines with them, Avery stared at the big board.

The space around them was clear. There'd been no activity at the wormhole.

He was sure that he and his people were right, that the Dusters' last "fleet" had been a final bit of desperation. There was no way anyone else was coming

But every time there was a pause in the action, he stared at the readings of the wormhole.

Sure, he was ninety-nine percent certain that no more Duster ships were coming through the wormhole. So were his tactical people, so was General Bauer, so was General Purvis.

Still, there was that other one percent. *What if we're wrong?*

"Firing solution received," said the navigator, Lieutenant Henry Brutsche.

"Plot a course, Lieutenant," Huse said.

Avery nodded in approval.

"Aye-aye, Sir," Brutsche said. Seconds later: "Course plotted and laid in, Sir."

The helm officer, Lieutenant Junior Grade John Mihalowski, stifled a yawn. He was usually on the second shift, but he had traded shifts at Captain Huse's recommendation once it became clear the Rod from God was being used.

Mihalowski, according to Huse, was the best pilot he'd ever seen. "The lieutenant could land *Durango* on the head of a pin," the captain had claimed, never mind that *Durango* wasn't even designed to land on a planet's surface. But it also had the spatiodynamics of a brick—it wasn't meant for precision flying, but if you wanted the Rod from God to hit a particular target, as opposed to just a general pounding of the surface, you needed your ship to be in a specific spot in geo-sync orbit. That took a pilot with ice water for blood, and Huse believed Mihalowski was that pilot.

"Helm," Huse said, "put us into position."

"Aye-aye, Captain," Mihalowski said through another yawn.

"We keeping you awake, Lieutenant?" Huse asked.

Mihalowski grinned. "Just barely, Sir."

The helm officer manipulated the thrusters in tandem to get *Durango* into the position dictated by Brutsche's course.

"Too much, Mihalowski, you're gonna overshoot," Brutsche muttered at one point, and Mihalowski heard him.

"No, I won't, Hank," Mihalowski said, "it'll be fine."

"It better be," Avery said.

Mihalowski swallowed. "Yes, Sir, Admiral!"

Brutsche shook his head. "It'll only be okay if you go the way I told you to go—and don't call me 'Hank.'"

"Soon's you pronounce Mihalowski right," the pilot said with another grin. Avery noted that the helm officer said, "me-uh-LOV-skee," as opposed to Brutsche, who pronounced it, "me-ha-LAU-skee."

Another thruster blast, and then Mihalowski said, "In position."

Finkenbiner said, "Confirmed, Durango at optimal position for orbital bombardment."

"Ready projectile," Huse said.

With a nod, Finkenbiner said, "Readying projectile."

Avery glanced at a corner of his big board, which showed the external camera by the bay door that was now opening. The Rod from God levered out until it was pointing straight downward at the atmosphere below.

"You're drifting, me-ha-LAU-skee," Brutsche said.

"I see it, I see it," Mihalowski muttered, firing another thruster.

This type of drift was common for so large a vessel as *Durango*, and also typically wasn't any kind of cause for concern, except during a docking maneuver—or when trying to fire the Rod from God to a precise target. Half a degree off course, and the projectile would hit the Marines four miles away—or the clearing four miles east—or the farms four miles west.

So Mihalowski had to keep this large, ungainly ship from drifting even a little bit. No mean feat when micrometeors heading toward Troy struck the hull, or when the gravitational pull of the planet itself tugged you off course.

Finkenbiner said, "Firing solution *not* optimal."

"Hang on, Chief, just got hit by a micrometeor," Mihalowski said. "Compensating."

"That did it," Finkenbiner said. "Firing solution optimal."

Avery turned to nod at Huse, who nodded back. "Fire projectile."

"Projectile away," Finkenbiner said.

On the screen, the Rod from God disengaged from its mooring and started to fall toward the planet lazily.

Checking his console, Finkenbiner said, "Projectile is on course for target."

"What's the time to impact, Chief?" Huse asked.

"Three hours, forty-eight minutes, Sir."

"Projectile on main screen," Avery said. *They all should see this.*

"Putting projectile on main screen, aye," Davis said.

The cameras on *Durango*'s outer hull were able to follow the Rod from God as it fell toward the stratosphere.

"Good work, people," Avery said.

Huse added, "Lieutenant Brutsche, plot us an orbital course that will bring us back over target three-and-three-quarter hours from now."

Brutsche smiled. "Already done, Sir, and sent to me-uh-LOV-skee."

Mihalowski turned and stared at the navigator in shock. "We been serving together six months, you finally get it right?"

"You finally earned it."

"Thanks, Hank."

That made Brutsche's smile fall. "Excuse me, but as everyone on this bridge is a witness, you said you'd stop calling me Hank when I pronounced your name right."

Mihalowski shrugged. "I lied."

Chuckles went around the bridge.

Normally, Avery and Huse would shut down such side talk, but they'd just performed an intense maneuver successfully, the results of which wouldn't be known for almost four hours.

More to the point, it was a planetside engagement, one that helped all the Marines and soldiers on the ground. It had, Avery knew, been a source of frustration to many of the sailors under his command—and, when the admiral was willing to admit it, to Avery himself—that the losses his own forces had taken had combined with the need to be vigilant against more space-bound attacks from the Dusters to make the Navy a non-factor in the terrestrial parts of this engagement. The loss of Task Force 7 meant that naval resources were stretched thin.

But this last engagement with the dregs of the Duster fleet indicated that that had changed.

The ground-pounders may think they can do it all themselves, but it goes a lot better when you've got your guardian angels in orbit, and we've got your backs now, Avery thought toward the surface.

Brutsche and Mihalowski were still going at it. "Damn pilots. No respect at all for the people who tell you where you're supposed to go."

"I'm glad after six months you finally figured *that* out." The cheeky grin Mihalowski said that with fell as he added, "Sir, orbital position now eighteen hundred miles and holding steady. ETA back at this spot is three hours, forty-one minutes."

Huse nodded. "Excellent work, both of you, which is why I'm going to forgive you squabbling like teenagers on the bridge of a Navy ship."

Both lieutenants swallowed audibly.

"Yes, Sir," Brutsche said quietly.

"Thank you, Captain," Mihalowski said in a more subdued voice than Avery had ever heard him use.

Avery gave Huse an approving nod and then said, "Captain Huse, come with me to my office, please."

Getting up from the center chair, Huse nodded to the watch commander, Lieutenant Commander Rufus Z. Johnston, who replaced him in the chair.

Upon entering the admiral's office, Avery went straight for the drinks cabinet and pulled out a bottle of single-barrel Jack Daniel's.

"Sir?" Huse prompted.

"It's almost four hours before we know what'll happen dirtside, Captain, and after all that, I need a damn drink."

"I see, Sir."

Avery then smiled as he pulled out two thick-bottomed glasses. "Drinking alone is a sign of depravity. So you're drinking with me."

Huse wasn't about to turn down Avery's quality booze. "Understood, Sir."

The admiral poured the amber liquid into each of the glasses and then handed one to Huse.

"To the Rod from God."

"To the Rod from God," Huse repeated and waited for Avery to sip his drink before he did likewise.

The alcohol burned pleasantly in both men's throats.

"Hope to hell it works," Avery muttered.

Huse let out a sigh. "Amen."

Outside Jordan

Specialist Baldonado was starting to wish he'd kept his mouth shut and just agreed with Specialist Yano that they couldn't program Romulus and Remus to work for them.

Because if he hadn't been so goddamn cocksure that he could dope out how to run the Duster vehicles, they wouldn't have sent him to babysit Romulus while the Marines used it against the Duster forces outside Jordan.

"We're giving Romulus to the Marines," Bacon had told the nerd squad. "They're letting us keep Remus for now, but we have to be ready to hand it over at a moment's notice if they need another big-ass gun."

"Understood," Alchesay had said.

"Who's coming to pick it up?" Yano had asked.

"We're bringing it to them—specifically," Bacon had then looked right at Baldonado, "you are, Joe. And you're gonna operate it."

Baldonado had put a hand to his chest in abject shock. "Me?"

"You're the one who knows the programming, and we need an Ace on standby in case it goes tits-up."

And so Joe Rodriguez Baldonado, specialist first class in the NAU Army, whose only fieldwork was building things before or after combat occurred, and who otherwise spent most of his time in laboratories, was going into battle with the reinforcements being sent to Jordan.

At this point, it wasn't a single company or platoon that was going, but all the able-bodies who could be spared. The firebases were either secured or destroyed, ditto the farm where they'd captured the eggs, but the losses had been hefty. Major Yeiki Kobashigawa had been tasked with assembling an ad hoc company to reinforce the soldiers and Marines at Jordan. Someone had nicknamed them Improv Company, and it had stuck.

"This is *not* what I signed up for," Baldonado muttered to himself as he walked behind Romulus, which rolled slowly across the ground outside Jordan toward where the fighting was.

"Thought you joined the *Army*, soldier," said Corporal Nantaje. He was the leader of Baldonado's Marine escort. The corporal had been assigned to protect the engineer, along with three PFCs, Jose M. Lopez, Alexander Mack, and John J. Tominac.

"I joined the Army Corps of Engineers. We're a non-combat unit."

"What idiot told you that?" Nantaje asked.

Shaking his head, Baldonado said, "My recruiting officer."

"Ah, that explains it. They lie like cheap rugs."

"Yeah," Lopez said, "they told me it was a place to build character."

Nantaje chuckled. "Lopez already was a character, so that was bullshit."

Mack added, "They told me it was good pay and great benefits, and let me tell you, I'd make more money in my Mom's business and better benefits, too."

Tominac didn't say anything, so Baldonado prompted him. "What they tell you, Private?"

Shrugging, Tominac said, "Didn't tell me nothin'. Just signed my ass up."

"The point is," Nantaje said, "what they tell you in recruiting is bullshit. Kinda like how the battle plan never survives engagement with the enemy."

"Got *that* shit right," Lopez said. "These alien motherfuckers weren't supposed to be this crazy."

"Neither were we," Baldonado said.

"What do you mean?" Nantaje asked.

Pointing at Romulus, Baldonado said, "According to the metric shitloads of paperwork we got with this thing, this is the first time the Dusters have used these suckers in one of their invasions of other worlds."

"Really?" Nantaje stared at Romulus. "Not any of the other seventeen times?"

"*Seventeen times*?" Lopez asked. "They done this shit before?"

"At least," Nantaje said.

Tominac shook his head. "Fuck me backwards, Lopez, don't you read the reports?"

"He started 'em," Mack said, "but his lips got tired."

Lopez shrugged. "Don't need to read 'em, Johnny, I got you to quote 'em at me chapter and motherfuckin' verse."

With a sigh, Tominac said, "We found seventeen planets that've been wiped out the same way the Dusters wiped this place out. But none of them have had any sign of things like Romulus here."

Lopez winced. "C'mon, man, don't be usin' that stupid Ace name."

"What's wrong with calling Romulus by name?" Baldonado asked.

"Just call it a fucking attack vehicle."

Baldonado shook his head. "You jarheads got no poetry in you."

"Fuck you, Ace, I got plenty'a poetry."

"Yeah," Mack said, "but they're all dirty limericks."

"Wait," Lopez said, "there's *other* kinds of poems?"

Nantaje was about to say something when his earpiece crackled with a single word from Sergeant Arthur F. Defranzos: "Mark."

The Marines all clammed up at that point. They were now at the spot where they needed to be ready to engage, as they were almost on top of the fighting. Now that he wasn't bantering with the Marines, Baldonado could hear the reports of weapons fire from both sides.

Whatever pleasant distraction the Marines' bullshitting had accomplished for Baldonado went right out the window once they shut up, because now Baldonado could hear his own death.

He tried not to tense every time he heard the report of weapons fire, especially since it meant he was constantly tensing.

Besides, he had a job to do. He was the programmer, and his task when Defranzos said, "Mark," was to run the second of two programs. The first was a simple roll-along, but now that they were about to engage, he had to run the second program: where

Romulus would fire the ten-thousand-megawatt weapon at regular intervals.

His original orders were to fire when instructed, but Baldonado had to admit to Major Kobashigawa that he couldn't.

"Explain yourself, Specialist," Kobashigawa had said in a tight voice.

"We've been able to figure out how to run the programs that are already in the system, but we haven't been able to reprogram them."

"So?"

Baldonado had sighed. He'd learned the hard way not to get too technical with non-engineers, especially ones not actually assigned to the Corps of Engineers. Marines, in particular, tended to get cranky when you over-explained. So he tamped down his lengthy diatribe about how it's easy to read the programs but not so much to rewrite them, and instead said, "Right now, the best we can do is do what the Dusters had it do: move and shoot occasionally."

"You can't control the weapons?" Kobashigawa had asked. "Then why do we even have this thing?"

"Uh, Sir, we can control it, but it's limited. We can tell it to fire every—" He had double-checked his control unit, then. "—forty-nine-point-four seconds because that's what the Dusters programmed it to do. I can't change the interval, I can just either have it *at* that interval or not fire at all."

Kobashigawa had sighed. "I repeat my question: if we can't control it that much, why have it?"

It was Sergeant Defranzos who had replied to that: "Sir, the weapon it fires is ten thousand megawatts. It wiped out most of our forces at the firebases."

The major had blinked several times, then had looked at Defranzos, then at Baldonado, then at Romulus. "All right, then," he had finally said before walking off.

Right now, the Marines of Improv Company were on either side of Romulus. Glancing around the side of the vehicle, Baldonado saw that the Marines whom they were reinforcing had adjusted position to the left and right so that they weren't in Romulus's line of fire.

The vehicle was going to fire in ten seconds.

The Dusters themselves were adjusting their fire, but also advancing through this unexpected hole in the Marines' line.

Oh, man, was that *a stupid idea.*

Nine seconds...

The Marines had made a V-shaped hole in the line, and were firing across the Dusters' flank.

Eight seconds...

In retaliation, the Dusters charged right forward, weapons blazing.

Seven seconds...

The Dusters' weapons fire bounced off Romulus the same way the NAU weaponry did at the firebases. If they were moved by the fact that their own weapon was being used against them, they didn't show it in any way that Baldonado could see.

Six seconds...

Mack was winged by Duster fire and fell to the ground.

Five seconds...

Baldonado swallowed audibly, realizing that the Dusters were getting very close now, and he suddenly wondered if the aliens were somehow immune to the weapon or if they had a way of controlling it that he and the rest of the Aces hadn't noticed.

Four seconds...

"Corpsman!" Mack was crying out.

Three seconds...

This was the first time Baldonado had seen the Dusters up close and personal. While he intellectually knew about their weird jinking motion when they traversed ground on foot, actually seeing it was a bizarre experience.

Two seconds...

He found he needed to look away before he got seasick.

One second...

The front of Romulus started to glow with a blinding luminescence. Looking down at his control unit, he saw the infrared scan that showed the giant arc of the ten-thousand-megawatt laser beam.

It stopped firing, and he peeked out from behind Romulus to see the result.

The Dusters that were still upright—which weren't many of them—were in total disarray. Some were still firing, but most were jinking back and forth in place and confused.

The ones that weren't dead, at least.

Thank Christ it worked, Baldonado thought.

"Move in!" came Defranzos's voice over general comms, and all the Marines moved forward, closing the hole once again, now with much greater numbers on their side.

On the discreet freq, Defranzo said, "Specialist Baldonado, discontinue firing and cease forward motion of Romulus."

"Um, okay. I mean, yeah."

He tapped several commands into his control unit. Seconds later, Romulus rumbled to a stop.

A Corpsman had arrived and knelt beside Mack, whipping out a pressure bandage.

"We gonna get in on the action?" Lopez asked Nantaje.

"Nice try, Private, but we stay here, make sure that nobody messes with our new truck. Our job is to protect it—and the specialist here—at all costs."

"Glad I made the cut," Baldonado muttered.

It only took a few minutes after that, but it was all over. The Dusters who survived Romulus's blast seemed to have been completely caught off-guard by the vehicle's attack.

Just as Baldonado was about to ask if he could turn Romulus around to bring it back to the Pork Barrel, he was stunned by a massive blast to the west.

Turning his head, he saw a huge explosion where the forest outside Shapland was supposed to be.

Admiral's Bridge, Durango

"Projectile has struck dead on target!" Chief Finkenbiner cried out as the Rod from God struck the forest with a massive impact.

Admiral Avery and Captain Huse nodded. Everyone else on board let out a single whoop of glee.

"Good work, sailors," Avery said. "Lieutenant Commander Davis, contact General Bauer and inform him that the Rod from God has done its job."

"Aye-aye, *Sir!*" Davis said with a grin.

"And ask for further orders. About time we got into the ground game."

Mathews Base Hospital, Millerton

Colonel Frances Cunningham had stepped outside for air. She stared up at the sign that was attached to the wall next to the doorway to the medical base. It was the second sign the base had had. The first had just read BASE HOSPITAL.

Then, during the earliest of the engagements with the Dusters after making planetfall, Georgia Mathews, one of Cunningham's medics, got shot while getting a comatose Marine to safety. She had refused treatment, insisting on getting the Marine to the ambulance, then going out and bandaging someone else's wounds instead of getting treatment for herself.

Eventually, she'd collapsed on the battlefield, but not until four soldiers and two more Marines were patched up and sent back to this very base hospital. And everyone she'd treated had made it back alive—unlike Mathews herself, who died from internal bleeding thanks to an untreated wound.

In the same tradition that led to the firebases being named after the fallen, Cunningham had had the base hospital renamed after Mathews, and the medic was for damn sure getting some kind of posthumous medal when this was all over. *Hell, if I have to steal a medal from the Prairie Palace itself, I'll do that,* she thought.

Cunningham hadn't been able to keep track of every single patient who had gone through the hospital, but she'd made sure to check on the status of the seven troops throughout the rest of the fighting. Two of the soldiers were wounded, but still at it, two of the Marines had been killed in later action—one in the field, one on the table in Cunningham's surgical unit—and the other two soldiers and one Marine had, so far, continued to survive.

Her gaze moved from the sign up to the sky. The sun had set, and it was a clear, cloudless night, so she saw tiny pricks of light that she figured were Navy vessels in orbit. Or maybe they were stars that were particularly bright—astronomy wasn't Cunningham's strong suit. Either way, they made for a pretty sky, whether or not they were faraway suns or close-by fighting ships.

Those fighting ships had, at least, provided a shipment of meds, which they sent down via the orbital elevator. She'd been two steps away from proscribing booze to ease her patients' pain for lack of anything better, and Cunningham really didn't want to be reduced to that. Besides the fact that it wasn't as effective, she didn't want to dip into her precious personal supply of single-malt Scotch.

An alarm sounded from inside the hospital, disturbing Cunningham's reverie. She went back inside to the main desk. "What's going on?" she asked Private Verna Baker, the clerk.

"Something's happening in quarantine, ma'am."

"Shit." That meant the Dusters, since no humans had been admitted to the Quarantine Unit in the rear wing of Mathews since the armed forces had arrived at Troy.

She moved quickly through the halls of the hospital to the QU, which consisted of ten large rooms, each with its own observation chamber.

In addition to the five Duster eggs that had been confiscated on the farm outside Jordan, they had been forced to put five of the prisoners into quarantine. The Duster prisoners—designated PW0015, PW0016, PW0018, PW0020, and PW00022—had all started secreting some kind of fluid.

The lab was still trying to figure out what that fluid *was*.

The eggs and prisoners had all been placed in Room 8. Going into Room 8's observation chamber, Cunningham saw that two of her other physicians, Major Allan Jay Kellogg and Captain Georgia Nee, were already there.

"What've we got?" Cunningham asked.

Kellogg pointed at the eggs, which were on the far side of the quarantine unit, sitting on tables.

Which, Cunningham noticed, were shaking. And one of them was cracked.

"Oh, great," she muttered. "They're hatching."

Nee shrugged. "We knew that was going to happen eventually."

"Yeah, but I really didn't want it to happen while the prisoners were still in there."

"We could've put them in a separate room," Nee said. "In fact, I said from jump that—"

Interrupting Nee harshly, Cunningham snapped, "I know what you said, Georgia, I was there. I know I was there because I rejected your proposal."

"For no good reason!"

"For *very* good reason!" Cunningham shook her head. "We've only got ten rooms in the QU, and if we put Dusters in *another* room, that's *two* we can't use anymore for our people."

Nee was insistent. "We haven't needed *any* for our people, much less eight—or nine. And it means there's no risk of cross-contamination between the eggs and the adults."

"We haven't needed any for our people *yet*, but that could change in a heartbeat, and I don't want any soldiers, sailors, or Marines dying of some delightfully exotic new alien disease because we didn't have enough room in the QU because *two* of the rooms were occupied by the aliens who murdered every living being on this planet. Am I clear, *Captain*, or do I need to explain again?"

Letting out a long sigh, and not looking nearly abashed enough to suit Cunningham, Nee said, "Yes, Ma'am."

Turning her back on Nee, Cunningham regarded Kellogg, who had stood very quietly during that harangue. "Do we have any idea what that damn fluid is that they're spitting out?"

Shaking his head, Kellogg said, "We do not. Unfortunately, it's gotten worse since we put them in there. It's specifically coating their extremities."

"Yeah, but—" Then suddenly something occurred to Cunningham. "Where did those prisoners come from?"

"What do you mean?" Kellogg asked.

Even as he asked that Nee was reaching for a comm unit.

"I mean," Cunningham said, "we've got a batch of prisoners the Navy took from the last engagement in space, and we've got a batch that came along with these eggs from the farm near Jordan. Which batch did these prisoners come from?"

Nee scrolled through the display. "Here it is—PW0015 through PW0023 were all brought in by Sergeant Ruiz."

"The farm." Cunningham blew out a breath and looked back at the eggs, which had now started to crack. "It's very possible that these particular Dusters laid these particular eggs." She shot a look at Nee. "All the more reason why we shouldn't separate them."

"We don't know that," Nee said petulantly.

"No, but as a general rule, living beings tend to be present when they produce offspring. I think we can play the percentages here and keep the parents with the kids."

"If they are the parents," Nee said. "They could—"

Kellogg interrupted. "They're hatching!"

A bit of shell broke off one egg, and a larger bit broke off another. Soon all five of them started to shed the shells.

Glancing to the side, Cunningham verified that the surveillance in Room 8 was functioning properly. This needed to be saved for evaluation.

"Can you believe this?" Nee asked. "We're seeing something no human has seen before. An actual alien birth."

"I'd be more impressed," Kellogg said, "if it was a nice alien birth."

"I make it a rule never to judge babies by their parents," Nee said.

Cunningham had to admit the woman had a point. Just because the Dusters they'd encountered were murdering bastards didn't mean they all were. And one of several reasons why she'd rejected the Catholic Church as a teenager—much to her parents' chagrin—was that she rejected as revolting the entire notion that all humans were born sinners.

For all that this was an alien birth, the process by which the eggs hatched was surprisingly mundane. The shell cracked and fell away to reveal a beige membrane, through which they could see indistinct shapes wriggling about.

One limb poked through the membrane of one egg, then another. Similar actions happened throughout the clutch.

The creature that came out looked nothing like the adult Dusters. They had light green skin, covered in a viscous fluid that probably had provided nutrients while inside the egg. The infants had no feathers, their limbs were comparatively stunted, and their bodies were quite skinny. They had the long necks of their adult counterparts, at least, and the long jaws that jutted forward from their heads.

As soon as they extricated themselves from the membranes, they jumped to the floor and immediately ran toward the adults.

For their parts, the five prisoners were sitting on the floor with their limbs all jutting forward, covered in the unidentified fluid.

And four of the infants started licking the fluid off the limbs. The fifth wandered around the room for a few minutes, then finally meandered toward the last remaining adult Duster, and also started licking the fluid off the limbs.

Cunningham glanced at Kellogg. "Allan, we have samples of that fluid, yes?"

"Yes, Ma'am."

"Get the lab to start trying to reproduce it. We may finally have something we can feed the prisoners."

"Colonel," Nee said, "with all due respect, that's like feeding mother's milk to a grownup."

"If it's the only food available, I'd do that in a heartbeat. At least we know it's something that will keep them from completely starving to death."

"I'll get right on that." Kellogg turned and left the observation room.

The five infants sat happily licking away. Meanwhile, the adults were making clicking noises.

Between gulps, the infants were making the same clicking noise back.

"Holy shit," Cunningham muttered.

"What is it, Ma'am?" Nee asked.

Ignoring her, Cunningham went to the intercom and contacted the front desk.

"Baker," the clerk said.

"Private, contact *Durango*, tell them they need to put their ship's linguist on the elevator down here ASAFP. Then get me General Bauer and tell him we've got Duster babies—and they're already talking."

Orbital Elevator descending to
McKinzie Elevator Base, Outside Millerton

PETTY OFFICER SECOND CLASS ISAAC L. FASSEUR RODE DOWN THE ORBITAL elevator to Troy with his stomach doing flip-flops and his heart beating like a triphammer.

"You all right, Ike?" Chief Petty Officer George Francis Henrechon asked him.

"No, I'm not all right! What the hell kinda question is that?"

Henrechon shrugged. "I woulda thought you'd be happy as a pig in shit, m'self. I mean—you're a xenolinguist, right?"

Fasseur rolled his eyes. "No, Chief, I'm the ship's cook, but I talk real good, so they assigned me to this duty."

That prompted a belly laugh from the chief, and a chuckle from Lieutenant Commander Benjamin Levy, who sat on the other side of Fasseur in the elevator.

"Well, frankly, Petty Officer Fasseur, I wouldn't put it past the great NAU Navy brass to assign a cook to this particular duty."

"Actually, Chief, I can't even boil water."

"Fine, then you really are a xenolinguist. So why aren't you all happy and stuff? I mean, school was a while ago, but I'm pretty sure they taught me that if you put 'xeno' in front of a word, that means 'alien,' which means that your specialty is alien languages, am I right?"

Fasseur nodded.

"So now you get to talk to an actual alien in its actual language. What's the problem?"

"How much time before we land?"

"Twenty minutes," Levy said.

Nodding again, Fasseur said, "I might have enough time." He took a deep breath. "Look, it's one thing to *study* alien languages. You've got a margin for error, and it's all theoretical. You write papers, you compare stories, you look at the big picture, you check all the different sources. Hell, for the last six weeks, all I've done is read over every damn thing from all seventeen sites where we've found evidence of Duster invasions, trying to find some damn thing that will give me a hint as to what their language is.

"But, y'see, that's the *easy* part. Research is safe. If you fuck up, nobody cares—well, that's not true, all the *other* linguists care, and they rip you to pieces, but that's just 'cause we all ripped *them* to pieces when *they* fucked up. But even that's useful because when you fuck up, you learn stuff.

"That's back home, though. In the field? Ain't no damn margin for error. I fuck this up, and I could make the war go on longer. Or at the very least get people killed. There are *stakes* now, you know what I'm saying? That's why I was so glad that Jimmy Mestrovich got this gig initially, may he rest in peace."

Petty Officer Second Class James I. Mestrovich was, like Fasseur, a xenolinguist, and he'd been assigned to *Durango* when they shipped out to Troy initially. He was also rated as a pilot, and after the initial engagement, he was called upon to fill in as copilot in one of the Meteors—which was then destroyed.

However, it quickly became clear that there wasn't a need for a xenolinguist on this mission. The Dusters had shown no interest in negotiating, no interest in *talking*, and given their actions, nobody in the NAU military was all that interested in having a conversation, either.

Now, though, they were at the talking stage. As he'd said to the chief, Fasseur had been assigned to study everything he could about the Dusters once hostilities kicked in, and now he was assigned to the latest batch of reinforcements.

"Coulda been worse," Henrechon said. "We coulda got here and had to fight our way to Troy. But it looks like the Dusters are pretty much toast."

"So are our forces," said the woman sitting across from them.

Fasseur had actually forgotten that the reporter was there. Florence Groberg had been sent along to report on the war for the folks back home, and when she learned that Fasseur was being ordered to make contact with the aliens via the prisoners they'd taken, she bullied her way into going along. She'd been sufficiently unobtrusive in her observations on the trip out here that she had blended into the background, which probably helped her do her job better, though Fasseur found it unnerving.

He'd also heard a rumor that she was a former Navy boat captain, though he wasn't sure he believed that.

Groberg continued: "The difference is, we still have reinforcements in reserve, while they seem to have run out. I got to talk to someone on *Durango* after we arrived, and the ships the Dusters sent through were rejected surplus."

"Which means they're ready to talk," Fasseur said, "but what if I get it wrong? What if they misunderstand us? What if I misunderstand them?" He shook his head. "I call myself a xenolinguist, but honestly? There isn't any such thing, because the field is so new and unknown and we haven't encountered enough other languages even to have a proper database, and—" He made a strangled noise. "It's just a mess."

"Maybe," Groberg said, "but it's all we got. Diplomacy happens either because you can't fight anymore or you don't want to fight in the first place."

"The second one was never the case here," Levy muttered.

Nodding, Groberg said, "Right, but the first case is now."

"Oh, I dunno," Henrechon said, "I'd be happy to keep fighting until all those fuckers are dead. Don't," the chief added quickly, "quote me on that! But I had friends who lived here on Troy."

"Nothing we're saying right now is on the record," Groberg said softly.

"Good, then I can say this to you, Ike: don't worry about it. Best case, you talk to these alien assholes, and we get a treaty in place, or at least a cease-fire, and we go our separate ways. Worst case—

well, like the reporter lady said, we got reinforcements, they don't. I like our odds if conversation don't work out so good."

Fasseur found he had nothing to say in response to that, and neither did anyone else.

And then the elevator started its deceleration, which would take up the final fifteen minutes. Fasseur's stomach went from flip-flops to out-and-out rebellion as the brakes were applied to the elevator. For a moment, he thought for sure he would throw up all over the deck.

Finally, the elevator came to a stop. Everyone undid their safety restraints before waiting for the announcement that the elevator was secure, and they could disembark.

Awaiting them was a small group of people in uniform, but only two stepped forward to greet them: a Marine with captain's bars and a soldier wearing a lab coat and a colonel's bird.

"Welcome to Troy," the captain said. "I'm Captain Upshur, General Bauer's aide, this is Colonel Cunningham, our chief medical officer."

Levy nodded. "I'm Lieutenant Levy, this is Chief Henrechon. I'll be taking care of the first batch of reinforcements."

Indicating a major who was standing nearby with a group of Marines, Upshur said, "Major Metzger will take care of you, Lieutenant."

Again, Levy nodded, and then said, "The chief here will be escorting Petty Officer Fasseur."

"You're the linguist?" Cunningham asked.

Fasseur nodded. "Yes, Ma'am."

"Then who's she?" She indicated Groberg with her head.

"Florence Groberg, *Omaha World-Herald*. I've been sent to tell the folks back home what's happening here."

Upshur snorted. "Hope that tablet has a *lot* of memory on it. You're gonna have plenty to write about, Ms. Groberg." He turned to Fasseur. "Chief Henrechon, Petty Officer Fasseur, you're both to come with the colonel and me to the base hospital. That's where we're holding the aliens, and you can start your work."

Upshur and Cunnigham led Fasseur, accompanied by Henrechon and Groberg, away from the elevator station, while Levy met up with Major Metzger to organize the distribution of the other elevator passengers, who were there to replace some of those who'd been killed in action.

As they walked toward the hospital, Fasseur asked, "Why are they in the hospital? Are they sick?"

"In quarantine," Cunningham said. "We've got some baby Dusters that just hatched." She quickly gave a rundown of the Dusters who were secreting the fluid and also the hatched eggs. "But that's not the fun part," she added. "It's what the babies are saying."

"They're talking already?"

"Oh, yes. Quite the chatterboxes, are they. And they're growing quick, too. Only been a couple days, and they've doubled their size. At this rate, they'll be the same size as the adults inside a week."

"Wow." Fasseur hadn't expected that.

"But that's not the interesting part." Cunningham smiled strangely when she said that.

"What do you mean?"

"You'll see."

Mathews Base Hospital

Florence Groberg wasn't sure what surprised her more: that Lieutenant General Harold Bauer, commander of the 1st Marine Combat Force and acting commander of NAU Forces his own self was in the observation room of Quarantine Unit #8, or that she was hearing words in English through the speakers.

The latter went some way toward explaining the former, as the early stages of this sort of diplomatic event would normally be beneath a three-star's notice.

But the only beings inside the QU were Dusters. And yet Groberg definitely was hearing English words coming over the speaker.

Most of what came from the speakers were clicks of varying lengths, but they were mixed in with more familiar words. Groberg caught "fluid," something that sounded like either "feeding" or "heeding," and "growth" amidst the clicks.

Upshur said, "Lieutenant General Bauer, this is Chief Henrechon, who's escorting our xenolinguist, Petty Officer Second Class Fasseur. The civilian is Florence Groberg—she's reporting on the war for the *Omaha World-Herald*."

Henrechon saluted to Bauer, but Fasseur was completely captivated by the aliens he saw through the window.

Bauer returned the chief's salute, then said, "This is Captain Nee, one of Colonel Cunningham's staff." He offered a hand to Groberg. "Pleasure to meet you, Ms. Groberg. I've always admired your work."

"Thank you, General," she said.

Then Bauer turned to Fasseur, who was still staring, open-mouthed, at the Dusters. "Never seen an alien before, Petty Officer Fasseur?"

Without even looking at the general, Fasseur said, "No, Sir, I haven't. They're—they're amazing."

Groberg wondered how Fasseur had managed to become a xenolinguist without encountering any aliens but said nothing.

"So amazing that they make protocol fly right out of your head, eh?" The general's tone was reproving, but friendly.

Shaking his head several times, Fasseur whirled around and quickly stood at attention and saluted. "Sir! Sorry, Sir!"

Returning the salute, Bauer said, "At ease, Petty Officer."

"Thank you, Sir," Fasseur said, sounding incredibly relieved. Bauer would have been within his rights to discipline the young man severely, but he was here for a very specific purpose that they needed to commence. "Sir," Fasseur said hesitantly, "they, um, speak English?"

"Not quite," Cunningham said. "But they've been picking up words and using them when they talk to the adults."

"And the adults are sticking with their language?"

Cunningham nodded.

"How much of their language have you been able to dope out?" Bauer asked.

"Not that much," Fasseur admitted. "They speak in what sound like clicks and dashes. It has a certain structural similarity to Morse Code, but it's not a one-to-one analog, obviously. They also seem to convey a lot of information through minimal words—kind of the verbal equivalent of certain pictographic languages that convey lengthy multisyllabic words with a single image."

Fasseur then hesitated, listening to the sounds coming from the QU.

Groberg also listened, mostly hearing the Duster words, but with "nutrients," "growth," "mobility," and "development" mixed in. She also noticed that the pronunciation was a bit odd. "Development" in particular sounded odd—more like "develonent." It seemed like any sound involving lips was hard for them to manage. But glottals and sibilants didn't seem to be an issue.

"Right." Fasseur turned to look at the Dusters. "Everything they're saying is a word that you, Colonel Cunningham, and you, Captain Nee, and any other medical personnel who were in here would have been using multiple times to describe their progress in there." He turned to Bauer. "Sir, I believe that the newborns are able to assimilate language from what they hear around them—same way we do as infants, but it seems to happen at a greatly accelerated rate with them, especially given that they're obviously already conversing with the adult Dusters."

"So, you're saying they may learn English?"

"I'm saying we need to make sure there are lots of conversations here. Maybe even speeches that have concepts we need them to understand and be familiar with so they can serve as translators for the adults."

Bauer turned to the reporter. "Ms. Groberg, how'd you like to help the war effort? Or, more to the point, the peace effort?"

"How's that, General?" Groberg asked though she had an inkling.

"I want you to work on that speech the petty officer was talking about with Captain Upshur here. I want these alien babies to hear all about diplomacy and treaties and terms of surrender—and also strength of reinforcements, if you get my drift."

Groberg smiled. "I do, General."

"Sir," Fasseur said, "with your permission, I'd like to stay and observe the aliens further."

"That was going to be my order, Petty Officer," Bauer said. "I want you to get to know these prisoners as best you can, and I especially want you to trust the newborns, since you'll be communicating with them. Let's get to it, people."

Article by Florence Groberg
in the Omaha World-Herald

Today, the guns are silent.

General Douglas MacArthur said those words at the end of the second World War on Earth in the twentieth century, and they also apply today on the Semi-Autonomous World of Troy, as the fighting that raged on this colony world has at last ceased.

The joint forces of the NAU military, including an Army division, two Navy task forces, and two Marine divisions, have fought a long and brutal battle here on Troy, though it is as nothing compared to the suffering of the people of Troy, which prompted the battle.

Without warning, without hesitation, the alien species that have come to be known as "Dusters" invaded Troy, leaving no one alive in the wake of their vicious assault.

This is not the first time that the so-called "Dusters," whose own name for themselves is unpronounceable by human tongues, have done this to a world. We have, in the years since we started colonizing space, found seventeen different worlds that showed the type of destruction and devastation wreaked upon Troy.

Unlike the other seventeen races that were demolished by the Dusters, however, the people of Troy had someone to avenge them.

The losses were devastating. Navy Task Force 7 was utterly wiped out, and Task Force 8 has suffered considerable losses in battles that took place in the space above Troy.

On Troy itself, thousands of Marines and soldiers have died, both on the ground and in the air. The Dusters have been relentless in their attacks, tunneling under the ground, engaging in brutal assaults across the terrain, and finally using a series of ground assault vehicles that fired lasers more powerful than anything seen on Earth or Troy.

But the Dusters reckoned without the fighting spirit of the NAU soldiers, sailors, and Marines.

They also reckoned without human ingenuity. According to several of the personnel interviewed by this reporter, one of the major turning points in the campaign was when NAU forces captured two of the Dusters' ground-assault vehicles and turned them over to the Army Corps of Engineers. The "Aces," as they're called, were able to reverse-engineer the vehicles and use them against the Dusters, helping to turn the tide of battle.

The forces here never forgot those who fell, but they also never lost sight of what they fell fighting for. Many of the structures here are named after the fallen—firebases renamed after Marines killed in action; the base hospital renamed after a medic who died saving the lives of multiple troops.

It was at the Mathews Base Hospital that the hostilities officially ended. By the time this reporter arrived on the scene with the second batch of reinforcements the NAU sent to Troy, there was very little fighting still going on—a few skirmishes here and there—but the Dusters seemed ready to surrender.

Dusters appear to be asexual, and they reproduce automatically. Several eggs laid at a farmhouse outside Jordan hatched to form a new set of Dusters. These, however, weren't fighters—at least not yet.

This reporter was privileged to observe these alien newborns in action. They quickly learned not only the Duster tongue of their forebears but also the human tongue that they heard while in the Quarantine Unit of the base hospital.

As it turns out, this was the method by which the Dusters intended to negotiate terms of surrender. They knew that their offspring would be able to learn our language and communicate with us, enabling us to draw up a treaty.

The Dusters ceded control of the Semi-Autonomous World of Troy back to the North American Union and also pledged to stay away from any world under Earth control. Any Duster ship seen approaching an Earth colony would be treated as hostile and fired upon. Unlike the invasion force that first attacked Troy, we now know what to look for, after all.

Normally, there would be some manner of reparations from the surrendering side. Either they would provide financial compensation for losses, or make an offer to assist in rebuilding. The Dusters seemed utterly baffled by this concept, and it soon became clear that this was not to be part of any negotiation.

This leaves the fate of the world of Troy up in the air. Only a fraction of the world's infrastructure is still in place, with most of it devastated, damaged, or destroyed. It's an open question whether or not the world will even *be* rebuilt, given the devastation. Especially with no help forthcoming from the Dusters.

It's not clear whether or not they have no concept of financial remuneration, no concept of finance at all, or if they do, but find the idea of reparations foreign. As much as the newborn Dusters were able to understand at least some of the English language, a lot of the concepts did not translate back and forth.

One of the unexpected bones of contention was over how the Dusters would retreat. Many of their space-faring vessels were damaged upon arrival by the Navy, and many more were shot down by NAU forces. Lieutenant General Harold Bauer, commander of the 1st Marine Combat Force and overall commander of the NAU Forces on Troy, felt that their casualties were high enough that their remaining vessels would be sufficient to the task. The Dusters, however, were insisting on having transport vessels brought in from their homeworld.

Negotiations on that particular point lasted the better part of a day and were in danger of growing contentious. It took considerable back-and-forth among the Dusters and with General Bauer and the Navy xenolinguist, Petty Officer Second Class Isaac Fasseur—who assisted in translating—before a compromise was *finally* reached. The Dusters will send one rescue vessel, to be escorted by a flotilla of

NAU Navy ships from the wormhole to Troy and back to the wormhole, along with the remaining spaceworthy Duster ships.

In addition, the Dusters wished to gift approximately a hundred eggs containing soon-to-be-born Dusters to the NAU as tribute to do with as they would. This reporter got the impression that they intended to hand over their newborns as slaves for us to exploit—or, possibly, spies to learn more about us for potential future incursions.

General Bauer politely declined that offer, which seemed to confuse the Dusters greatly. The general did not wish to raise the security concerns specifically, and they did not seem to understand that slavery is very much against the law in the NAU. At Petty Officer Fasseur's suggestion, General Bauer explained to them that integrating their people into our society would cause more problems than it would solve.

Once the negotiations were concluded, official statements were made by both sides. Petty Officer Fasseur read the following statement, which he helped the Duster newborns put together on their behalf:

"We wish to express our admiration and respect for the human battlers who have fought us to defeat. Never in the history of our worlds have we fought a foe as valiant or as tenacious. In particular, we are impressed with the human battlers' ability to commandeer our battle vehicular conveyance for their own use against us."

After that, General Bauer made his official statement on behalf of the forces under his command:

"We have fought hard and paid a dear price, but in the end, we were victorious. We have shown that human ingenuity, stubbornness, pride, skill, and determination will win the day. We have shown that we will not tolerate an invasion of our homes, that we will not tolerate the wholesale slaughter of our people. We can be friendly and tolerant people, but we will not be abused, we will not be crossed, and we will not be victims. The fine Marines and sailors and soldiers—the fine human beings who make up my command here on Troy have excelled themselves against a vicious, brutal foe who gave no quarter. And we gave none back. Our losses were significant, but they did not give their lives in vain. An invader that would surely have turned their attention to another colony world next, or even to Earth itself, was instead shown the door. Our primary mandate is to protect the people of the NAU and the people of the human race, and when we can't protect them—as, sadly, we could not protect the people of Troy—then our secondary mandate is to avenge the fallen, which we have done here. The Dusters will think twice before crossing the people of Earth again."

EPILOGUE

William F. Lukes Memorial Park, Shapland,
Semi-Autonomous World Troy

STAFF SERGEANT J. HENRY DENIG STOOD WITH MOST OF THE ABLE-BODIED soldiers, sailors, and Marines left on Troy. They had assembled in the large park in the center of Shapland that had been hastily renamed after the late President of Troy, who had died in the Dusters' initial invasion.

Right next to him were the rest of Force Recon first squad: Sergeant Edward Walker, Corporal John Rannahan, Corporal Charles Brown, and Lance Corporal Erwin Boydson.

They watched as Lieutenant General Bauer, Admiral Avery, and Major General Conrad Noll, the commanders of the Marines, Navy, and Army, respectively, on Troy took their places facing them all. Avery held some kind of control in his left hand.

Between the three commanders and the troops stood a brazier.

Bauer stepped forward. "I'm not one for long speeches—the lengthy harangue that was in the *World-Herald* notwithstanding."

Denig chuckled, as did several of the personnel gathered.

"But I do want to say this: We lost a lot of good people in this war. I won't insult your intelligence by saying I knew every Marine who died, and Admiral Avery and General Noll can't say the same about the sailors and soldiers they commanded. For that matter, few if any of us really knew the people of Troy personally. We can't stand here and eulogize all of them, much as we would wish to. The sheer numbers are overwhelming—but so were the odds that we would win this war.

"And so, rather than try to memorialize everyone individually, we choose instead to memorialize everyone collectively."

General Noll stepped forward. "Specialist?"

Willa Alchesay from the Army Corps of Engineers stepped out of the crowd and walked up to the brazier. She touched a control on the side, and then a huge flame bloomed from within. The flames licked high toward the sky.

Noll looked out at the assembled multitudes. "The Army Corps of Engineers has put together this eternal flame that will burn in this park forever. We don't know yet what the future holds for the world of Troy—that's for the folks back home to decide. But no matter what will be on this world in the future, this flame will continue to burn in memory of those who fell, both the civilians and military personnel who died in the initial invasion and the people under our command who died in response to that invasion." Noll reached into a pocket and pulled out a metal plate. "We will now affix this plaque so future generations will know what happened here—what we lost and what we gained."

The general placed the plaque on the side of the brazier.

He then stood at attention.

Off to the side—Denig couldn't tell who—cried out, "*Comp*-ney, ten-*HUT!*"

Everyone came to attention.

Bauer, Avery, and Noll all looked at the brazier and saluted.

The entire complement assembled saluted as well.

"Rest in peace." Bauer whispered the words, but everyone heard them.

The three commanders finished their salutes, as did everyone else a moment later.

Avery held up the control in his left hand and pressed a button.

Moments later, fireworks blazed in the sky above.

A susurrus of "ooh" and "aahhh!" spread through the personnel gathered as the colored lights burst through the twilight sky.

"Courtesy of *Durango*," Avery said with a proud smile.

"Excuse me, Staff Sergeant Denig?"

Turning, Denig saw a woman in civilian clothing. She must have come with the latest wave of reinforcements, and he wondered what a civvie was doing here. "Yes?"

She held out a hand. "Florence Groberg, *Omaha World-Herald*. I've been sent to cover the war and its aftermath."

"Um, okay." Denig returned the handshake out of politeness, but he had very little use for journalists. Still, he wasn't about to be rude. "What can I do for you?"

"I've actually been looking for you for a while. Sergeant Ruiz says you were part of the team that first scouted out the farm where the eggs came from?"

Frowning, Denig said, "Among other things. Why?"

"I've been talking to everyone who was on or near that farm. It was owned by a man named George B. Turner. He came here to start up his own farm, along with his family. There was one family member, though, who wasn't able to come out with them initially, as she had obligations back on Earth, working on a project. But that project was almost finished, and she was getting ready to head to Troy to join the farm. Obviously, that's not going to happen."

"Okay." Denig really hoped the reporter would get to the point soon.

"I talked to Day Turner before I came here, and she mentioned a snow globe that she'd sent to George last Christmas."

And now it all came together. "Holy shit."

Groberg tensed, and spoke with a hopeful lilt in her voice. "You know what I'm talking about?"

Nodding, Denig reached into the pocket where he'd placed the damaged snow globe. "It's not in the best shape. I found it on the ground near the farm. Honestly, not sure why I kept it, I guess—" He glanced at the eternal flame. "I guess I wanted to memorialize the people here." He turned to face Groberg. "I suppose you want to bring it back to her?"

"It would mean a great deal," Groberg said emphatically. "She honestly didn't expect anyone to find it, and I didn't think anyone would. I was just asking on the off-chance. You found it on the ground?"

Denig nodded. "Under a tree. Here." He handed it to her. "And—and tell her I'm sorry, and—and Merry Christmas."

Groberg smiled and wrapped the snowglobe in a cloth before placing it in her pack. "Thank you, Sergeant. You've done a good deed today. Now, if you'll excuse me, I have to talk to Specialist Alchesay. I've been promised a detailed description of how they reverse-engineered the Dusters' tanks."

"Hope you budgeted an hour," Denig said with a snort. "The Aces tend to get a little long-winded."

"That's what editing is for, Sergeant. Thanks again." She offered another handshake.

This time, Denig returned it with more enthusiasm.

As Groberg went to talk to Alchesaday, Rannahan clapped Denig on the back. "Jesus, J. Henry, you really are a softie, ain'tcha?"

"Kiss my entire ass, Corporal."

First Lieutenant John A. Hughes walked up to them and said, "All right, Marines, playtime's over. We've still got a shit-ton of work to do. There are some Dusters *and* our own people and equipment that are unaccounted for, and nobody sniffs out what needs sniffing better than Force Recon. So let's get back to work!"

Denig said, "Oo-rah, Force Recon!"

All the Marines standing before Hughes repeated, *"Oo-rah, Force Recon!"*

And then they got back to work.

THE END

ABOUT THE AUTHORS

DAVID SHERMAN IS THE AUTHOR OR CO-AUTHOR OF SOME THREE DOZEN BOOKS, most of which are, like this trilogy, about Marines in combat. He has written about U.S. Marines in Vietnam (the *Night Fighters* series and three other novels), and the *DemonTech* series about Marines in a fantasy world.

Other than military, he wrote a non-conventional vampire novel, *The Hunt*, and a mystery, *Dead Man's Chest*. He has also released a collection of short fiction and nonfiction from early in his writing career, *Sherman's Shorts; the Beginnings*.

With Dan Cragg, he wrote the popular *Starfist* series and its spin-off series, *Starfist: Force Recon*—all about Marines in the twenty-fifth century—and a *Star Wars* novel, *Jedi Trial*. His books have been translated into Czech, Polish, German, and Japanese.

After going to war as a U.S. Marine infantryman, and spending decades writing about young men at war, he's burnt out on the subject and has finally come home. Today he's writing short fiction, mostly steampunk, and farcical fantastic Westerns.

He lives in sunny South Florida, where he doesn't have to worry about hypothermia or snow-shoveling-induced heart attacks. He invites readers to visit his website, novelier.com.

KEITH R.A. DECANDIDO IS A WRITER AND EDITOR OF MORE THAN THREE decades' standing (though he usually does them sitting down). He is the author of more than 50 novels, more than 100 short stories, around 75 comic books, and more nonfiction than he is really willing to count. Included in those credits is fiction in the worlds of *Star Trek, Alien, Farscape, Doctor Who, Andromeda, BattleTech*, and many other science fiction milieus, as well as in universes of his own creation (such as the "Precinct" series of fantasy police procedurals, also published by the fine folks at eSpec). As an editor, he has worked with dozens of authors, among them Mike W. Barr, Alfred Bester, Margaret Wander Bonanno, Adam-Troy Castro, Peter David, Diane Duane, Harlan Ellison, Tony Isabella, Stan Lee, Tanith Lee, David Mack, David Michelinie, Andre Norton, Robert Silverberg, Dean Wesley Smith, S.P. Somtow, Harry Turtledove, Chelsea Quinn Yarbro, and Roger Zelazny.

Having edited David Sherman's first two 18th Race books, *Issue in Doubt* and *In All Directions*, he is honored to assist in finishing the trilogy by coauthoring *To Hell and Regroup* with him. Keith is also a martial artist (he got his third-degree black belt in karate in 2017), a musician (currently with the parody band Boogie Knights), and a baseball fan (having avidly followed the New York Yankees since 1976). Find out less about Keith as his cheerfully retro web site at DeCandido.net.

PATRIOTIC SUPPORTERS

A. Parsons
Allyn Gibson
Amy Laurens
Andrew Corvin
Andrew Glazier
Andrew Timson
Andy Hunter
Anonymous
Ashli Tingle
Barb and Carl Kesner
beardedzilla
Bradij
Brenda Cooper
Brendan Lonehawk
Brian D Lambert
Brian Griffin
C. Frost
C.A. Rowland
Caleb Monroe
Carol Gyzander
Carol Jones
Carol Mammano
Charname
Chelsea Provencher
Cheri Kannarr
Chris Matthews
Christopher D. Abbott
Christopher J. Burke
Christopher J. Ford
Christopher Thompson
Chuck Wilson
Cody Steinman
Craig "Stevo" Stephenson
Dale A. Russell
Daniel Lin
Danielle Ackley-McPhail
Danny Chamberlin
David Holden
Dawfydd Kelly
Diánna Martin
Dominic
Donald J. Bingle
Dr Douglas Vaughan
Dr. Karen
Eli Berg-Maas
Eli Mellen
Emily Weed Baisch
Eron Wyngarde
Evan Ladouceur
Frankie B
Gary Vandegrift
Gavin
GraceAnne DeCandido
Håkon Gaut
Hiram G Wells
Howard J. Bampton
Ian Harvey
Idran
Isaac 'Will It Work' Dansicker
J Paulus
J. B. Burbidge
Jakub Narębski
James Flux

James Goetsch
Jaq Greenspon
Jeff Metzner
Jeff Singer
Jennifer L. Pierce
Jeremy Bottroff
Johanna Rothman
John Green
John Idlor
Joseph Charpak
Josh Vidmar
Josh Ward
Judith Waidlich
Keith West, Future Potentate of the Solar System
Kelly Pierce
Kerry aka Trouble
Kierin Fox
Kyle Franklin
Lark Cunningham
Larry
Leon W. Fairley
Lewis Phillips
Lisa Hawkridge
Lisa Kruse
Lorraine J. Anderson
MaGnUs
Malcolm Eckel
Margaret M. St. John
Maria T
Mark Beaulieu
Mary Catelynn Cunningham
mdtommyd
me@edmondkoo.com
Michael Brooker
Michael Doyle
Mike M.
Ms. Dyane Stillman
Nathan Turner
Norman Jaffe
Pam DeLuca
Patrick Foster
Paul van Oven
Peter D Engebos
Phillip Thorne
PJ Kimbell
Pulse Publishing
Ralph M.Seibel
Richard P Clark
Richard Todd
RKBookman
Robert C Flipse
Robert Claney
Robert M. Sutton
Samara N. Lipman
Scott Crick
Scott DeRuby
Scott Mantooth
Scott Schaper
Serge Broom
Shane "Asharon" Sylvia
Sharon Abdel-Malek
Shervyn
Sheryl R. Hayes
Stacy Butcher
Stephanie Souders
Stephen Ballentine
Stephen Lesnik
Steven Callen
Stoney
The Amazing Maurice
The Creative Fund
Thierry Millié
Tim DuBois
Tom B.
ToniAnn Marini
Tony Hernandez
V Hartman DiSanto
Vince Kindfuller
Wayne Garmil
William C. Tracy
Zeb Berryman